Someone was shaking me. Hard.

"LaTisha?"

"What you doing? I'm awake." I peeled my eyes open and focused on Hardy's anxious face. My head felt all cottony.

"Tish, something awful's happened. You gotta come downstairs with me. She's dead."

I blinked and pushed the recliner's footrest down. Hardy didn't look so good. His eyes rolled around so much I could see the whites, a sure sign he was scared. That's when his last couple of words registered. My heart clenched. "Who's dead?"

Surely not my mother-in-law. . .

"Polly Dent. Seems she had a bad fall on the tread-mill. She's dead."

Other mysteries by S. Dionne Moore

Murder on the Ol' Bunions

HEARTSONG
PRESENTS
MYSTERIES

Polly Dent Loses Grip
A LaTisha Barnhart Mystery

S. Dionne Moore

For David. Every day with you is an incredible gift of love and commitment, faith and fun. I love you.

Huge thanks to Imogene Folt (LPN), Tiffany Sounders (CNA), as well as the staff at The Children's Institute, Pittsburgh, especially Roberta (RN) and Linda (LPN), for helping me with my research in the long weeks we were there. Any mistakes are my own.

Cover design: Kirk DouPonce, DogEared Design
Cover illustration: Jody Williams

Our mission is to publish and distribute inspirational products offering exceptional value and biblical encouragement to the masses.

Printed in the U.S.A.

1

A sea of gray-headed residents, in various stages of nap time, greeted me and my husband, Hardy, as we made our way toward the elevators of Bridgeton Towers Assisted Living & Nursing. Blue walls with one of them fancy rail things halfway down and green paint below, echoed the colors of the carpet. Couldn't see much else on account of the mattress I was carrying.

Besides a few more boxes, we had almost moved Hardy's momma, Matilda, into her new home. We'd be spending a week trying to help her get settled in and decorated up before we headed back to our hometown in Maple Gap, Colorado.

"Hurry up, LaTisha. You know how Momma doesn't like to wait."

I shot my husband the hairy eyeball. "You thinking I don't know that by now? And if you're in such a hurry, why don't you hightail your hind end up the stairs instead of waiting on an elevator?" I hiked the twin mattress higher on my hip and hustled my way faster toward the elevator.

Hardy's a lot like a bantam rooster, and since he's *my* husband, I can make such comparisons. Shorter than me by about six inches, he's as thin as I am . . . Um. Next subject.

As his hair has grayed, it's gotten to where it likes to fuzz up like bad Velcro. I'll have to get that boy to the barber, and by the looks of him, sooner than later. The elevator dinged, and the doors slid open. Hardy hauled his box spring straight toward the doors, cheeks all puffed out like it weighed a ton. Reminder—*I had the mattress.*

He'd drifted out of my line of vision, on account of the mattress glued to my hip, but I heard him shuffling and grunting.

"What you doing?" I pursed my lips and repositioned my grip on the mattress. "Get yourself settled and tell me when—"

"Don't get your hose in a twist. I'm hurrying."

A few of the residents were waking, looking over at the elevator with curious eyes. I let the mattress slide to the ground to inspect why some were cracking smiles. Hardy'd tried to move sideways and was now wedged in the elevator by the stuck box spring. Never in my life. . . Seven children together and this man was still the biggest one of them all.

I leaned the mattress against a table and lent Hardy a hand. He flashed me a near-toothless smile of gratitude as I gave the box spring a yank and shove that whizzed it right into place. Mission accomplished, I stroked my hand along his head.

A giggle alerted me to the presence of a little gal with a walker, peering around the corner at us.

"Got yourself a fan club."

I gave the little lady a wide smile.

"Mirzi," she screeched in a high-pitched voice.

"Name's Mirzi Mullins."

"How do you do, Miss Mullins? My mother-in-law's moving in today, Room 207. Come by and we'll visit."

Mirzi's bright eyes shone for a second before she

nodded and trundled herself toward a corridor. "Let me get Gertrude. If I can get her to move her feet, she's the one who you'll want to meet."

While I'd had my back turned, Hardy had gotten it into his head to slide the mattress into the elevator by himself. I crossed my arms and watched as he grunted and groaned, tugged and pushed. He's cute to watch. Pitiful but cute.

He backed up a pace. Two. I knew his methods. He was going to hurl himself at the thing in hopes of body-slamming it inside. Like a bull scratching the dust—I could almost see the steam coming out his nostrils as he flung himself forward and promptly bounced backward right onto his rump.

His eyes darted at me. I grunted at him, relented, and gave the bulky thing a mighty heave that sent it slipping right into the elevator. Hardy hopped in after me and punched the button for the second floor, waving as the doors closed to all the residents so entertained by our little display. I even heard a few clapping.

Hardy's momma waited for us, face set in stone, leaning hard on her cane, as the doors slid open like curtains on the first act of a play. And Matilda Barnhart is quite the character, let me tell you. Recent victim of a stroke that left her weak on her right side, she's doing a whole lot better, thankfully, but after enduring months of physical therapy to get strong—and me praying for God's grace to *be* strong while she was with us during her recuperation—we all decided the time had come for her to be on her own again. She wouldn't be solo anymore though, giving up her old apartment and agreeing to a future in an assisted-living environment.

Knowing someone would be here to check in on her gave Hardy the peace of mind he needed, and being on her own gave Matilda the independence she wanted.

If Hardy is a little guy, his momma is even smaller. But I never underestimate those ninety-eight pounds.

"Thought you'd done gone to sleep on my bed," Matilda spat out.

See what I mean? "No, ma'am," I assured her.

Hardy mumbled something from behind the box spring he was pulling from the elevator. He nearly bowled his momma over when he turned the corner, one end of the box spring bearing down on her hard and fast. She did an awkward two-step with her cane and glowered at his back, mumbling what sounded like, "That boy trying to kill me?"

I followed Hardy, turning the corner, my arms spread wide around the mattress, and had a straight shot of the long hallway. Momma's room, third door on the left, was wide open, and I saw the back of Hardy disappear inside, seconds before a white-haired bun-head blocked the doorway, her back to me, and peered into the room. Since my cheek was plastered to the mattress, I couldn't turn my head to see if Matilda was close on my heels or not. Maybe she already knew this lady.

"Hey, you, whoever you are, you'd better get out of *my* apartment!" Bun-Head screeched at the top of her lungs.

She must have seen Hardy slip into Matilda's apartment. And, since she now blocked the entrance, I let my mattress slide to the floor, wondering if I'd ever get this thing to where it needed to be. "You lookin' for someone?"

Her sharp brown eyes lasered down the length of me. I felt the burn from head to toe. "You the new resident? You're stealing my apartment."

New resident? That scared me. "My name's LaTisha Barnhart." Hardy popped out of Momma's doorway, eyeball-to-eyeball with Bun-Head. "That's my husband, Hardy." I pointed at Matilda. "That's his momma, the new resident, Mrs. Matilda Barnhart."

Hardy pursed his lips, studying our visitor real close. "My wife just *looks* like she belongs here."

Bun-Head crossed her skinny arms. "Well, this is my room, and I want it."

Matilda caught up to us, paused to tilt her head at the visitor, then chugged forward, giving Bun-Head a chance to retreat a step or get steamrolled.

"You hear me?" Bun-Head threatened as Matilda closed the distance between them. "You better get your scrawny self out of my apartment. Otis promised me this place."

Now, not much gets Hardy riled, but you can guarantee he wasn't having Bun-Head say much more without his tongue doing some wagging. I watched as his posture changed from relaxed to alert. His eyes took on a feral gleam. "I'm sure there's a way to get this resolved without you calling my momma names, Ms. . . ."

"It's Dent. Mrs. Polly Dent." But those words didn't come from the little lady; they came from somewhere over my shoulder. Otis Payne, director of Administration for Bridgeton Towers and one of the people we met when filling out all that paperwork to get Momma into the facility, huffed up to us. His beady eyes and thin, strawberry blond hair lent him the look of a sunburned pig. Probably not such a nice way to describe him, but I couldn't help the impression or the comparison, Lord forgive me.

Otis's voice stopped Momma in her tracks long enough for her to give him the barest of nods. She then slid past Bun-Head and through the door. She never did say a word to Bun-Head. Must have been her hearing. Selective hearing, that is. Not a thing wrong with her ears otherwise.

Polly, who watched Momma blaze a trail to her bedroom, snapped her head toward Otis. "I can speak for myself."

"Yes, Mrs. Dent, I'm sure you can."

Otis jutted a hand out to Hardy. "Good to see you again, Mr. Barnhart." He then said something in a voice so low I couldn't catch the words, but his glance at Mrs. Dent let me know for sure who he was whispering about.

Whatever they said, Hardy nodded. Otis turned to me and moved to help with the mattress. I stopped him cold. "Good of you to offer, but I made it this far without help."

Polly snorted, and Otis turned her way. "Don't you forget our agreement, Otis Payne."

Otis's smile stretched from ear to ear, but it was 100 percent pure plastic. Before he could say a word, Polly spun on her heel and scampered down the hall like a Chihuahua dog who thought her bark had everyone scattering for cover.

"You get that mattress in here so I can lay these bones down," Momma hollered from inside the apartment. "I'm tired."

Hmph. Lots of scripture verses floated through my head about respecting one's elders before I dared even open my mouth. Just when things were getting good and a dozen questions had popped into my mind to ask Otis, too. I gave a mighty heave and slid the mattress inside her apartment. "Coming, Momma, dear."

It didn't take too long to settle Momma down after I'd dressed up the bed for her. Neither Hardy nor Otis were anywhere to be found. Strange thing, that.

Instead of searching for them, I opted to bring in more boxes. As I slipped into the hall, I heard a soft scraping sound and looked around to place the source of the noise. Across the hall, someone peered with one eye through the crack of a partially opened door. When our gazes met, the door shut fast-like. A curious neighbor who probably heard Polly screeching and wondered if the sky was falling.

I rode the elevator down, mentally reviewing the scene Bun-Head had created, and wondered if it was a taste of what Momma would have to face on a daily basis.

The rear of our car sagged low from the weight of all Momma's things. At least Hardy had disconnected the trailer so I could get to the trunk. I lifted out a box that clanked with the kitchen things she'd need— plates, forks, glasses, pots and pans. Like me, she loved to cook, although she didn't have to if she didn't want to since all her meals would be prepared for her at Bridgeton Towers.

I shouldered the box and rear-ended the door shut. And that's when I met Gertrude Hermann.

"That's why your car's so beat up."

I fastened my eyes on the large woman at the front

door, Mitzi at her side holding tight to her walker.

"Did the same thing. Car was dented all over. Course my car was a new model. Name's Gertrude Hermann." She nodded over at Mitzi and held the door for me as I neared. "This here is—"

"Already told her." Mitzi clanged her walker forward. "I've got a mouth of my own, ya know, Gertie."

Gertrude frowned. How'd these two stay friends? For the second time that day, I reeled off the pertinent details. No, I'm not a resident. Yes, my mother-in-law is settled in her apartment, room 207 to be exact. And yes, the short black man is my husband, Hardy.

Gertrude's voice stirred some of the slumbering residents as we entered the community room and headed toward the elevators. The doors swished open upon our approach, and out stepped none other than Polly Dent, with a tall, slightly stooped man, leaning on a gold-headed cane, at her side.

"Thomas, dear!" Gertrude gave a little shimmy of excitement. For a woman of her, uh, voluminousness, it wasn't a pretty sight. Like a stone in water. Lotsa ripples. "You going for a walk?"

The man waited for Polly to precede him off the elevator before sending Gertrude a tolerant smile. "It's lunchtime. Would you care to join us?"

Gertrude's lower lip protruded. Polly laid a hand on Thomas's arm, her eyes issuing a challenge to Gertrude. For sure, all was not sweetness and light between these two.

I stepped onto the elevator. Mitzi followed, muttering, but Gertrude held the doors open with her hand. She pointed toward me. "Thomas, have you met Mrs. Branstarch? Her mother's moving in—"

"To my apartment," Polly finished. "I've already been assured by Mr. Payne that my name is on the list for that room."

Thomas stared between the two women a minute before he stepped forward, hand extended toward me. "I'm sure your mother will enjoy living here."

"Please, call me LaTisha."

"A lovely name."

His breath came out in a cloud of minty freshness. Nice. And I could see where these two ladies would be addled over such a man. Charm. Warmth. Septuagenarian cute. But I had work to do, and more than anything, I wanted to drag Gertie into the elevator and get on up to Momma's apartment so I could have some things put away before she woke from her nap.

Gertrude leaned into Thomas as he withdrew, clinging to his arm a moment. "Thanks for inviting me. I'll be down shortly." She paused a beat and sent Polly a saccharine smile. "Why don't we make it a foursome by inviting Mr. Payne? He and Polly seemed so comfortable with each other last night. I'm sure he'd adore the opportunity to spend more time with her."

Classic catfight. Polly's claws extended, and lightning flashed in her eyes. That is, until Thomas's head swiveled her direction. Her glare smeared into a polite, if a little tight, smile.

Gertrude backpedaled into the elevator, waved at Polly and Thomas like Miss America newly crowned, and jammed her thumb on the CLOSE DOOR button.

2

Hardy slipped into Momma's room as I finished unpacking the last box. Just like a man. "Where you been? I've unloaded all these boxes by myself."

He cocked his hip and struck a pose. "Notice anything different?"

"Your hip out of joint?"

"No." He lifted his chin higher, holding his Mr. Universe pose.

I stared at the golf ball–sized muscle in his bicep. Hadn't grown one iota since I married him. When he went to carry me over the threshold after our wedding, I had to keep one foot on the floor to help him out.

I took a step closer to him. With his head angled backward, I did notice one thing. "Another limb has sprouted."

His posture shriveled. The prospect of another tree branch sprouting from his nose always humbled Hardy. He glared at me and stroked a finger under his nose. "How does that stuff grow so fast? I bushwhacked 'em three nights ago."

"Is that what you wanted me to notice?"

He plucked at his ears. "Got any new ones in here?"

I looked. "Nope." He disappeared into Momma's spare room. "You gonna answer me or not? What you come strutting in here for me to notice?"

He reappeared with his nose-hair clippers. "They've got a great exercise room, so I tried it out." He moved into the bathroom.

I couldn't bear to watch. I shut the door. Some things are just personal.

"I hope they have an aide in that gym." I could only imagine all those shuffling feet and weakened limbs straining and stressing. Sounded like a good way to get sued.

"The trainer was closing for the day as I left. Someone's always in there during hours. She told me I was in great shape."

My eyes crossed in exasperation. So that's what all this was about. Based on what this attendant lady sees on a daily basis, I could agree. "Probably says that to everyone."

He flung open the door. "You don't think I look good?"

"Oh, honey, you sure do look fine. And you're all mine." I lost the sweet tone and wagged my finger at him. "And don't you be forgetting it."

He grinned. "Just making sure you're noticing."

I put a hand out to balance myself, feeling suddenly exhausted. I'd probably overdone it again. It never failed to irk me how my body protested what my mind said I could do. I sagged against the door frame.

Hardy touched my arm. "You don't look so good, LaTisha. Sit down. I'll finish cleaning up this mess."

The extrawide recliner felt good. Jerking the thing off the trailer, into the building, and up to this room had been a job for two people. I should have waited for Hardy, but the dolly had helped, though the maintenance man could have offered a hand instead of being content to suck on that cigarette.

"Where'd you run off to after visiting the workout

room?" I asked Hardy.

"Mr. Payne had told me to drop by later, so I did. He wanted time to check his records and make sure there wasn't a mix-up with that apartment being double booked. There wasn't, and he said he'd have a talk with Polly." He wiggled his fingers. "Guess what I found. They got a piano in that downstairs common area. Kawai. Didn't sound too bad to my ear, so I spent awhile at the piano taking requests from the residents, then I saw Polly with Mr. Payne near the cafeteria. I decided to go have my talk with Mrs. Dent. By the time I got there, she was in the gym, mumbling something about people being tested or late or something."

"Thought you said it was closed."

"It was. Closes at two." He shrugged. "Anyway, I told her I'd talked to Mr. Payne. She kind of gave me a weird look and flicked on the treadmill without saying a word. I'm thinking she's not going to take this lying down."

Hardy stood where I'd left him, eyes roving over all the boxes and knickknacks. This boy needed some direction. "You can start by taking those boxes out of here. And you need to be telling me what you and Otis were whispering about after Polly finished shouting at Momma that this was her apartment."

He lifted the stack. "Just said she sometimes gets confused." He balanced the stack and with his free hand tugged open the door, letting his foot swing it wide. Next thing I knew, boxes were slipping and his arms were flailing. In the settling dust, I spied a petite young Asian woman, hand covering her mouth, a large metal cart separating her from the doorway. She yanked the cart aside and rushed to help Hardy to his feet.

"Oh, sir, please excuse. I'm so sorry to leave the cart out where you trip."

Hardy rebounded quite well. "It just startled me, and I tripped on the carpet when I stepped back." He gathered his boxes with the little nurse's help, but I saw the telltale raspberry tint on his chocolate skin.

She angled the cart so Hardy could pass, plucked up a cup of pudding, and walked it over to me. "This is your snack, Mrs. Barnhart. If you need help, you can call on the button in your room." She tapped her name tag. SUSAN MIE.

Hardy paused long enough to look at me with an expression that said he wanted to erupt in laughter.

You know, I was beginning to get a complex. Maybe I should do those microbraids after all. I sure didn't feel as old as I apparently looked. And Hardy—I was gonna jerk a knot on his head—I heard him howling the whole way down the hall.

Deep breath. Count to ten. "Honey, I'll be good and sure the resident gets this. Her name is Matilda Barnhart. I'm her daughter-in-law."

Sue Mie's eyes widened. "Please to know. I am sorry." She uncapped a pen and made a note on a piece of paper. With another nod and quick smile, she shoved her cart forward to the next door and knocked. I heard her call out, "Snack time."

I decided I'd best move the car out from guest parking, but when I tried to get to my feet, my sight got swimmy. Beads of sweat burst out on my forehead. I collapsed back in the chair. On second thought, I'd stay put for a few minutes, at least until Hardy got back.

⸺

Someone was shaking me. *Hard.*

"LaTisha?"

"What you doing? I'm awake." I peeled my eyes open and focused on Hardy's anxious face. My head felt all cottony.

"Tish, something awful's happened. You gotta come downstairs with me. She's dead."

I blinked and pushed the recliner's footrest down. Hardy didn't look so good. His eyes rolled around so much I could see the whites, a sure sign he was scared. That's when his last couple of words registered. My heart clenched. "Who's dead?"

Surely not my mother-in-law. . .

"Polly Dent. Seems she had a bad fall on the treadmill. She's dead."

It took me a second to place the name with the face—the scrappy little woman demanding this room. "You find her?"

"No. Mitzi Mullins did. I was coming back from the Dumpster and saw Mitzi. Her face was real white. . . ."

His complexion faded from dark chocolate to milk, and he swayed on his feet. I got up and pushed him down in the recliner real quick-like. He'd passed out on me before after laying eyes on a dead body, and I wasn't inclined to haul his limp carcass around to a doctor's office. "The police or someone here yet?"

He shrugged. "The on-duty nurse called the staff

doctor and Mr. Payne." Hardy raised his desperate gaze to mine. "What if they heard me and Polly arguing in the gym and think I did it?"

3

"You gonna look?" Hardy's voice trembled as he popped his head up over my shoulder then ducked again. The slim, vertical window in the door leading into the gym limited my view.

"No. I'm standing here with my eyes closed. What do you think I'm doing?"

"Is she moving?"

"Not a mite. Can't see much of her though. A foot. . .the left side of her body. . .powdery stuff on the floor. . .treadmills. . .water cooler. . ."

"You going in?"

You crazy? I didn't feel too great. My legs were all quivery, but it wouldn't do any good to get in a state. If I lost it, Hardy'd melt into a puddle. He didn't do blood, guts, or dead bodies, especially when the three were united. I turned away from the door and tugged him along. "Let's go talk to Mr. Payne. I'm wondering why the police aren't here yet."

We backtracked past a closed door to the next room, where Mr. Payne's secretary, Miss Pillsbury, sat shuffling papers. She appeared appropriately harried and concerned, given the dead body down the hall.

Images of the Pillsbury Doughboy with a wig and a few more curves came to me as I greeted the buxom woman with pencil-thin lips and heavy makeup. *Pillsbury Doughboy goes drag.*

Her eyes cruised the length and breadth of me, which took a few seconds since I wasn't exactly scrawny.

"I need to see Mr. Payne, honey. It's about Polly Dent."

Her red lips spread, smoothing the wrinkles that let me know just how painful this woman found it to be happy. "If you'll be seated, I'll call our director of administration and make sure he isn't in an appointment."

"Aren't you his secretary?"

Her smile dimmed a few watts. "Yes, I am."

"Then how is it you don't know if he's in a meeting or not?"

"I do take care of his appointments, ma'am, but he also has another entrance into his office that he sometimes uses. In this case of emergency, I'm sure you understand, he is very busy. If you'll wait a moment, I'll check to see if he's in."

Hardy poked his head around me. "Got any vending machines around here?"

For sure, that meant Hardy felt better. If he was thinking about his stomach, then I knew he'd be okay. Guess him knowin' I was handling things helped, too.

Miss Pillsbury shook her head. "I'm sorry. I can brew you a cup of coffee if you'd like."

I was ready to tell her to get on with her checking on Mr. Payne's appointments when Hardy piped up with, "Nah, we don't need that blood on our hands."

Miss Pillsbury's smile flatlined. "I'm sorry?"

Even I had to look over and wonder if my man had lost his mind. Maybe his hawked-high plaid pants were making him short of breath.

Hardy flashed his gold tooth at Miss Pillsbury. "Don't you read your Bible? It's not for a woman to be making coffee."

I caught on real quick. Hardy's humor was in high gear. Poor Miss Pillsbury.

Miss Pillsbury cleared her throat. "I don't drink it myself."

"Shine the light around us, brother," I encouraged, so we could get it over with.

"It's the Bible. *He*-brews." He bent double and slapped his leg, laughing himself stupid. I shifted my gaze to Miss Pillsbury, who looked downright scared, like God might send down some smoke bombs or something.

I winced. "We need to get your medication changed."

Hardy swiped his sleeve across his mouth as he straightened, releasing a final chuckle. "I don't take anything."

"Maybe we should start some, then."

Miss Pillsbury skidded backward in her chair and looked through the doorway into Otis Payne's office. Smile plastered, she motioned us inside and shut the door behind us.

Otis Payne got to his feet and extended his hand in greeting. I absorbed the decor—dark desk, huge potted plant, and to the right of his desk, cushioned chairs and a sofa—and the door that led to the hallway Miss Pillsbury spoke of, presently shut.

Hardy beat me to the punch. "We want to know why the police aren't here."

"You do get right to the point, don't you, Mr. Barnhart?"

"We do," I replied. "And we expect you to do the same."

"Fair enough." He nodded. "I didn't call them."

When I pressed him to explain, he worked the already loose knot of his tie. "It was an accident, I'm sure. We'll investigate why she was in the gym after hours, but the media would follow a call to the police and try to make a big deal of it."

Hardy and I sat side by side on the leather sofa across from Otis's desk. I put on my indignant face. "You've got a dead body not three doors down, and you're worried about the media?"

"It was an accident, Mrs. Barnhart, and I know what the police will do. They'll examine all the nursing records and question residents. In short, it'll create an uproar—"

"A panic, you mean."

He conceded the point with a nod. "Yes. A panic. In order to ensure some control over the damage done and to protect the residents, I'm going to do my own interviewing and look over the patient charts. Dr. Kwan, our staff doctor, will arrive shortly to examine the body himself."

"I'll call the police myself," I threatened.

Otis Payne's eyes slid over to Hardy. "There is your husband to consider. He was very upset over Polly's accusation and name calling. Did you tell Mrs. Dent about our discussion, Mr. Barnhart?"

This man was ruffling my feathers, for sure. "He did talk to her. Right there in the gym where she fell flat, and he has nothing to hide from the police. Leave him out of this."

"I'm only suggesting—"

"I know exactly what you're suggesting, and I'm telling you that you can leave my husband out of this.

Just because he and Polly had words doesn't mean he killed her." I lifted a hand to rub the back of Hardy's head. "Besides, he couldn't hurt a fly, poor scrawny thing."

Hardy came to life, nodding his head and flexing his golf ball muscle. "She's right. Wouldn't hurt a thing if I could and can't anyway. Tisha'll tell you I'm not a man."

"Not *the* man," I corrected him.

Otis didn't flinch. "I think you're misunderstanding me."

"I don't think so," I said.

Hardy's leg started to jiggle, his hand rubbing up and down his thigh. I reached over and stilled his hand, twining my fingers through his. The gesture wasn't lost on Otis Payne.

Hardy's free hand covered mine. "I saw her in the gym. She was mumbling something at first, then I told her what you said, Mr. Payne. She got on the treadmill and started yelling. I got out of there real fast before I said something I didn't mean. I didn't do anything."

Otis gave the simplest nod of his head, like somehow he wasn't convinced. He fidgeted with a pencil—bite marks evident all along the eraser tip. My boy Shakespeare did that. Awful habit. Never could use his pencils for long because the eraser got eaten. Come to think of it, he did have an awful lot of stomachaches in his school days. Got cured of the habit though. He bit into the eraser once and got jabbed in the jaw with a splinter. Had to take him to the dentist to get it removed, and if there's one thing Shakespeare hated more than liver, it was going to the dentist. Course, me and the dentist had a good talk before he ever extracted that splinter. A *good* talk. Dentist took his own sweet time extracting that splinter—mostly so he could lecture on pencil chewing. I'm thinking maybe I'd have to tell Mr. Payne the story.

"You sure she was in there after hours?" I asked.

"Yes." Hardy cocked his head to the side. "I did find it strange that she was in there after they'd closed, without an attendant. Isn't it supposed to be locked?"

I raised a brow at the director.

Otis started shuffling papers on his desk. "If it's a member of my staff, he or she will be penalized accordingly."

"Is there another entrance to the gym? Who has access? And the powdery stuff, what's that?"

"They use baby powder to keep their hands dry while working out. Recommended by our physical therapist." He cleared his throat. "Mrs. Barnhart, I can appreciate your concern over this matter, but I assure you I will take care of this in a satisfactory manner."

Hardy squeezed my hand. He knew I was working up to prime grilling temperature. There was Momma to consider. If this place wasn't safe, we had to know. "Sounds to me like I should be getting on that phone right this minute and calling those police."

Another squeeze. Harder this time.

"I'll meet them at the door and march them right into this office."

Otis's lips firmed into a straight line. "Please, Mrs. Barnhart, let me investigate. That's all I'm asking. Fatal falls are common in the elderly. Another resident had a fatal fall a couple of years ago."

"In the exercise room?" Sounded to me like he'd

better shut that thing down, or he'd be laying head-stones with epitaphs that spoke of happy lives lived to the fullest, until exercise killed them good and gone.

"No. This man fell in a hallway."

I turned to Hardy. "Maybe this isn't the best place to have Momma."

"I assure you, Mrs. Barnhart, I take all precautions necessary to protect—"

"Then you best be getting to the bottom of this. At least the police would set everything straight."

"I won't have them traipsing through my building asking their questions until I've had time to secure details from my staff. An accident is an accident. Nobody is accusing anyone of foul play—"

"You just pointed your finger at my man, Mr. Payne."

"A mere slip of the tongue. Really, there is no reason to think of Mrs. Dent's fall in such a suspicious light."

"What makes you so sure?" I slipped the question in.

Hardy leaned forward. "If it wasn't an accident, Mr. Payne, LaTisha's your woman. She feels crime. Almost has her degree in police science. You might have read of her last case in Maple Gap's newspaper about. . ." His face scrunched in concentration. "What? Eleven months ago?"

Otis's hands fluttered to his tie where they seesawed the knot. "If we need you, I'm sure your help would be appreciated."

Yeah, and I can lose a hundred pounds in a day.

A knock on the door interrupted Hardy's flapping gums, and there appeared in the doorway the little lady who had delivered snacks earlier. Susan Mie's dark ponytail slithered along her back as she hurried into the room, saluting us with a wan smile as she passed. "You want I should talk, Mr. Payne?"

"I did, Sue. I hope you brought your records."

She held up a sheaf of papers. "Something there is wrong?"

"There might be." He cleared his throat. "We—"

Another knock on the door and Gertrude stuck her head in. "Dr. Kwan's here. Is there something going on in the gym?" Her eyes swept over us. "Or maybe there's a party and I'm missing it?"

I took my time eyeballing Otis as he worked to placate Gertrude. He didn't appear put off by the woman's interruption or loud voice. As a matter of fact, he spoke to her with a calmness and lack of tie straightening that I found rather curious. He didn't let on that Polly was dead though, blabbing some drivel about a problem with the equipment.

"Well, okay. Thomas and I are taking a walk together. He does so love to exercise." She flashed a smug grin at me. One of those victorious grins. "He's probably waiting on me now."

"Good evening to you, Gertrude." Otis gave his nod of dismissal.

Gertrude turned with the speed of a sail barge, then she paused to glance back over her shoulder at Mr. Payne. "I'm looking forward to the banquet. It'll be wonderful to see your wife again. She's such a sympathetic listener."

Sure, and anyone listening to Gertrude would feel everyone's sympathy. *Jesus, forgive me.* Truth be told, people probably say such things of me, so I should give the woman a chance.

Otis offered a plastic smile. "My wife is looking forward to the event."

Now that was a bald-faced lie. Not only did Otis drum his fingers, but his eye contact was poor, and those are sure body language signs that a lie is being spun. Gertrude, however, didn't seem to notice and left without further comment—a minor miracle, to say the least.

Through all this, Sue Mie stood quietly off to the left, eyes on Mr. Payne. As his attention followed Gertrude's exit, her stare pierced him like a hundred needles.

Sweet Sue Mie might end up being a tigress in sheepskin. Her peripheral vision must have caught me watching. She shifted her head in my direction, the hardness in her expression melting so completely I almost questioned whether I'd truly seen it or not. But I had.

Otis blinked back to attention and held out an expectant hand toward Sue. "I'm researching all the angles, just to make sure everything is as it should be."

She handed over the files. "You not call an outside doctor? EMT? Police?" Not just an observation, to be sure—her tone had the edge of shattered glass. My brain heated. Sue Mie wasn't the least bit wary facing her boss, making me sure she had nothing to hide. But why the attitude?

Mr. Payne didn't seem to notice. He shoved piles of papers away from the center of his desk, set the file down, and opened it, his eyes zigzagging over the page. This was my chance to ask Sue Mie a couple of questions. I'd rather get my impressions of the situation from the horse's mouth than look over a dry report.

"Did you see Mrs. Dent this afternoon?"

Sue's eyes grew cautious, as if she were hiding something. "Of course. She my patient."

I'd have to win this girl's confidence if I was going to get anywhere. She clearly wasn't the trusting type, but why did she seem so guileless a minute ago when handing over her records? A strange mix.

"My wife is kind of an armchair detective." Hardy rolled his body forward, patting my leg. "You could say she's an inguesstigator of sorts."

In-guess-ti-ga-tor. I liked it.

He continued. "She and I captured the man who murdered Marion Peters over in Maple Gap."

Sue gaped, obviously making some mental connection. "You Barnhead lady?"

Hardy slapped his leg and guffawed. "Her head ain't quite that big."

I cocked my arm and gave him a good jab. He straightened up right quick. "You better shut your big trap before I knock that last tooth down your throat. You'll really be digging for gold then."

Otis cleared his throat. "Mrs. Barnhart will be helping me with the interviews."

Really? He'd had a mighty quick change of heart. It would make things easier for me to be able to talk freely to the staff. Given Otis's vow that Polly's fall was an accident, maybe his letting me look into it was his admission there might be more to the whole "accident." I wondered if something in Sue Mie's report had made him change his mind. I plowed right ahead with a question, before Otis did another flip-flop.

I bestowed my sweetest smile on Miss Mie. "Did Mrs. Dent seem well when you saw her this afternoon?"

Sue gave a single nod. "I knocked on door and gave snack."

"Anything strange about her behavior?"

She wilted against the wall. "She seems upset."

"What was she wearing?"

I could tell that Sue Mie was feeling the pressure

of the questions. Nothing like having to remember the details of someone's appearance when seeing them every day had become routine. She shrugged on a sigh. "I not know."

Mr. Payne glanced down at the papers, running a finger along a passage. "It says here Mrs. Dent was diabetic. You were aware of that as you dispensed the snacks?"

"I check records for all patients, Mr. Payne."

"I don't doubt that," Otis pressed, "but accidents do happen, and the police will double-check my notes on the matter once they are called in, not to mention the investigation the Joint Committee will also conduct. You might have dispensed the wrong snack."

A mistake that could cost Sue Mie her job, I figured.

Sue Mie's back seemed to stiffen. "Mrs. Dent is no my enemy."

There it was again. That hardness of tone, the flat stare, almost a challenge.

Mr. Payne steepled his fingers. "It is an easy *mistake* to make, Miss Mie."

She dropped her gaze. "Yes, sir."

If Otis Payne had sensed Sue's hostility, he didn't let on. Hardy shifted beside me and leaned to whisper. "I'm wondering what Mr. Payne was doing this afternoon."

That's what I love about this man; he fills in the holes of my thinking. Two halves that make a whole, that's us. Volleying a question at Mr. Payne would also give Sue a much-needed break, time to organize her thoughts a bit.

"In all this flurry of questioning, Mr. Payne, we'd like to know what you were doing this afternoon. Can anyone vouch for you?"

I can tell you right now he didn't like the tables being turned on him. The knot of his tie received another yank. An electronic *buzz* ripped through the silence and made him jump. He swiped a hand across his forehead. "Excuse me." And he lifted the receiver of the phone on his desk. "Hello, Otis Payne here."

He listened, his head resting in the cradle of his hand. "Yes, I'm aware of that, dear. This isn't a good time; I've had a very trying day." He stood abruptly, sending his wheeled office chair careening backward toward the wall and swung away, his back toward us.

I motioned for Sue to have a seat next to me and sent Hardy a meaningful look.

"What?" he asked.

"This girl needs to sit down," I hinted.

He assessed the small space on my other side. "Not all three of us is going to fit. Why don't you get up?"

"This is your opportunity to be a *gentleman*." Pink packets of sugar couldn't have been sweeter than my words or tone.

"You always telling me I'm not one. Don't see any reason to break that winning streak."

I lowered my voice for Hardy's ears. "Get your tail up out of here, or I'm gonna sit myself down on your lap."

He flashed his gold tooth at me. "Promise?"

"To break you?" I folded my arms. "Yup, I promise." Sometimes he acts like a young buck in rut, and I have to remind him that rut for him is nothing but a deep furrow in the ground.

He hitched himself to his feet and sank down in the armchair, the insufferable grin I loved so much still in place.

Otis's fervent whispers said the conversation wasn't going well. "You ever met Mrs. Payne?" I whispered to Sue.

"She come to dinners. She not talk much, especially not to residents."

If Otis's jerky actions interpreted the conversation, he was not a happy man. Apparently Mrs. Payne lived up to her name. His voice was low and abrupt, and then he spun toward us and jabbed the phone down onto its base. His eyes strayed toward the clock on the wall before he addressed us. "I need to conduct some interviews. Perhaps we can finish this conversation later."

Sue Mie and Hardy both took the dismissal and got to their feet. When I didn't move an inch, Hardy stared down at me as if I had a bomb strapped to my forehead.

"He means we need to get, LaTisha."

"He means *you* need to leave." I locked eyes with Otis. "But he invited me to stay for the interviews."

"I'm sorry, Mrs. Barnhart. There are things I need to take care of in private. You can feel free to talk to the residents. Maybe they saw something."

He'd backtracked pretty quick from wanting me to help in staff interviews. Maybe I was getting too close to something? "So you're admitting to the possibility that Polly's fall might not have been an accident."

Hardy's head rotated right and left between the two of us. "While you two sort this out, I'm going to check on Momma." He skedaddled out of there real fast, shooing Sue Mie in front of him, leaving me to face down Otis Payne.

Otis leaned forward, hands clasped on the desk.

"Mrs. Barnhart, you must understand something. I am approaching this investigation like it was an accident, not from the perspective that Mrs. Dent's demise was planned, plotted, or otherwise. There is no evidence in that direction."

I rolled back and forth on the sofa in an effort to get vertical. Drat these deep sofas. I finally got my feet under me. "Then you'll feel no threat if I look into this matter on my own. For my peace of mind."

Otis twitched. Or to be more precise, his eye twitched. He sawed at his tie a bit, then he cleared his throat. "If you feel you need to do this, I'm sure I can't stop you—"

I nodded. "You're seeing the light now, honey."

"Please exercise caution though. I don't want my staff pestered and distracted from doing their jobs correctly."

"And if you happen to be thinking Polly's fall wasn't an accident, I want Hardy left alone. The police start sniffing around him, and I'm going to make good and sure they know Hardy saw you with Polly this afternoon as well. You feeling me?"

His smile was tight when I left his office. Probably safe for me to assume that he would not be applying for a LaTisha Barnhart Fan Club card.

I determined to poke into the minds of the residents to see if anyone had noticed anything unusual about Mrs. Dent's behavior. I smiled my way through a couple of vague conversations with residents who had obviously seen nothing but the backs of their eyelids all afternoon. That's when my mind tripped across a familiar face. Mitzi Mullins shuffled a deck of playing cards and set up for a game of solitaire. I wondered if Gertrude had forgotten her friend; the little lady sitting here seemed a terribly lonely figure.

"Mitzi, did Gertrude return from her walk yet? Does she play cards with you?"

"Can't play solitaire in a pair."

Touché. "Did you see Mrs. Dent earlier today? Before her fall?"

Her silver head bowed over the cards, and it was impossible to see her expression. I watched as she drew from the pile and added to the rows, slow but sure, marveling at her concentration. But the longer I sat there, the more I wondered if Mitzi Mullins was clear minded. Her lips began to move, and her head bobbed, only slightly at first, then with more exaggerated motion as her voice became a whisper.

". . .at the door. . .on the floor. . .play fair. . .game of solitaire."

She smiled at me, her head going the whole time.

"Excuse me?" I asked.

This time I heard her loud and clear. "A dark shadow at the door. Polly Dent on the floor. Not everyone plays fair. Life for him is solitaire."

The rhyme rolled through my brain again. I stared at Mitzi as a bite of cold teeth sank into my spine. Were these ideas conjured from the dark recesses of her mind, or had Mitzi seen something?

Naw.

I mentally repeated the words with her as she repeated the rhyme, head still going back and forth. The strange feeling gripped me that my head was bobbing in time with hers. This was foolishness. I scooted back my chair. She didn't seem to notice at all, her hands moving steadily over the deck, laying out cards in order. She was well on her way to winning her game of solitaire.

5

There was no help for it. I was going to have to rule my nerves and go into the exercise room with old Polly girl. It'd help settle my mind to get a gander at Polly up close. The idea repelled me though—thoughts of Marion Peters, you know. The way I found her in her antique store all those months ago swam around in my head, making me dizzy and twisting my stomach into knots. At this rate, about ten years from now, I might be able to do this for a living. It made me wish I'd never decided to go into police science. The science part intrigued me, but the reality that prompted that part, not so much.

Polly's fall might have been an accident, but I didn't like the idea of an elderly woman in the gym by herself, falling and dying. Hardy and I at least owed it to Momma to make sure Bridgeton Towers righted whatever wrong had allowed Polly access to a place where she could put such a hurtin' on herself. Still, my brain buzzed that a fall like that shouldn't cause someone to die. A broken leg, hip—something like that—but death?

As I neared Otis's office area, I noticed the door leading from the hallway into his office was open. I walked right in. He wasn't there, so I decided to turn on the high beams and give myself a guided tour. His office wasn't overly huge, but it definitely showed signs of a working man. Garbage filled the trash can, and papers stuck out of a file drawer. His nice, tall plant turned out to be plastic and off center in the pot, guarding a door that appeared seldom used. I tried the door. It was locked tight. I tried to straighten the trunk of the tree and found it shifted easily in the pot. I left it alone to examine the bookcase. It held everything from popular fiction to law and medical books.

With nothing else to grab my interest, I sank down into the sofa, feeling like I was falling into a great pit. They had lift chairs, why not lift sofas? Sure would be convenient in a place like this where old knees and hips had a hard time working in sync with each other.

It didn't take long for Otis to make his appearance. He yanked his tie completely off as he shut the door behind him, never even glancing my direction. He mopped his face against his forearm. Seeing him so unnerved made me wish I could hide somewhere and spy on him. Had he worked up such a sweat interviewing people? Maybe he'd discovered someone had made a serious mistake and was sweating being found out by the police or the Department of Public Welfare or the Joint Commission.

"You feeling all right, Mr. Payne?"

To say that he jumped was a gross understatement. He couldn't have produced more thrust if he'd been a rocket launcher.

He blinked rapidly. "What do you want?"

Not the kindest conversation starter, but I'd cut the man a break. "Is Mitzi Mullins all here?" I tapped my head to clarify my question.

He slumped into his seat. "Early dementia."

"Can you let me in to see Polly?"

He frowned at me. "Why on earth do you want to see her?"

"To look at the scene before the police get here."

He bounced his fingertips on the table and exhaled. "Yes." He kind of hissed that last letter. "But don't touch anything. Don't even get close to her."

"Gertrude said Dr. Kwan had arrived. He look over Polly yet?"

Otis's brow creased. "Arrive?" Then his brow cleared. "Why, yes, Dr. Kwan is here. He's already seen the body."

Seemed mighty fast examining to my mind, but I kept that to myself. A doctor I'm not, so how would I know? Besides, Otis had neatly sidestepped something, and I had a mind to poke at him a bit on the subject.

"You never answered my question earlier. Where were you around the time of Polly's fall?"

He let out a long, slow breath. "Early dinner in the cafeteria. Mrs. Broumhild can verify that. I was in there the whole time."

"Didn't Hardy say he'd seen you with Polly?"

Otis flinched. "Did he? Probably before I went in for my late dinner."

I'd check it out just to be sure. But later. All I really wanted to do right now was get into that room and get it over with.

He thrust himself to his feet and motioned me to follow, looking a little rabid eyed, if you know what I mean. If he didn't calm down, he might have a heart attack.

As soon as Otis's hand rested on the doorknob of the exercise room, I braced myself. I averted my eyes from Polly as much as possible, scanning the area around the treadmill. The air held a certain unpleasant scent, precursor of what was to come should Polly remain in the room.

Otis toyed with his key, lips tightly pressed together. "Why don't I shut the door and wait for you out here? That way I can make sure no one interrupts. Don't get too close—I'll watch you through the glass."

Was that a warning? I put my hands on my hips and faced him square on—message sent.

He sucked in a breath, gulped, then backpedaled out the door. Message received.

Breathing a prayer for strength, I began to process each area, noting the lay of the equipment, the floor, the towel rack, a pan of white powder next to a dirty-clothes hamper. A couple of chairs, purple vinyl, if you can stomach the thought of that. A small trash can filled with paper cups from the watercooler and some powdery residue.

I retreated a few steps until my back touched the door to the room, blocking old Otis's view, though not on purpose. Mirrors covered the entire right and rear walls of the room, with a watercooler in the corner closest to a rack of towels.

I processed the area around Polly first, easing myself into looking her over, starting with the treadmill she'd fallen from. Identical to the other two in every way, including the presence of white powder on the handgrips and sprinkles apparent on the carpet. The baby powder, I guessed. The belt of Polly's treadmill had a chunk taken out of it on the right side; the belts on all three of the machines looked well worn. The emergency key dangled from Polly's hand. On the other two machines, the key was held in place by a little plastic shelf. Seemed normal enough, though exercise gave me the hives and the idea of having an intimate relationship with a treadmill or any other device of torture went contrary to my slogan of eat, drink, and be buried. Not that I imbibed anything stouter than grape juice, mind you, but good food was at the top of my list.

Except right here and right now, as my eyes turned to look over the body. My stomach clenched hard.

Polly's foot rested on the lower portion of the treadmill, as it had been earlier. I shifted my weight, sucked in a breath, quelled a gag, and forced myself to do a quick check of the rest of her body. My change in position revealed the glint of something metallic close to Polly's left hand but not quite hidden by the edge of the neighboring treadmill. Something I hadn't seen in my quick look through the window earlier.

I edged closer and squinted to see. It looked like a gum wrapper. I glanced over my shoulder. Otis's face pressed up to the glass, his eyes missing nothing. I gave a little wave and sauntered a couple of steps closer.

He pecked a warning on the glass.

Stuff it. I was going to find out about that wrapper one way or another.

Another step brought me within reaching distance, my mind spinning, trying to grasp a good excuse to use so I could grab that wrapper. If I bent over, Otis would barrel through that door and drag me out thinking I was up to something. Was he really that worried about disturbing the scene, or was it my presence that had him on edge?

I decided to use the old got-a-scratch excuse. It was lame, but when hose battle against the hairs on my legs, itching happens. Besides, it was all I could think up. I pretended to really be giving Polly the once over, though my eyes were on that wrapper the entire time. Then, when I'd done enough playacting, I bent over. Problem is, petite is not happening with this body, and my hands only made it to my kneecap. My hose rebelled against the pressure and tidal waved downward. No choice but to ignore that problem and do a scratch. Time was wasting.

I sure could use Gertrude or Hardy or Matilda showing up in the hallway about now and distracting my observer. But that didn't happen. A deep, masculine voice happened. I could hear Otis carrying on the conversation through the doorway. Their voices lowered a notch. They could whisper away, because Otis wouldn't be carrying on a conversation unless he was facing the person. Translation: He wasn't looking my way anymore.

I seized the opportunity to squat down and grab that wrapper with as much speed as I could muster. The muscles in the back of my thighs screamed a protest. I'd certainly pay the price tomorrow.

I held the wrapper to my nose—the faint scent of peppermint. Looked like those old Tic Tac Silvers wrappers from a couple years ago. Might mean something. Might not. I let it fall from my fingertips, disappointed, and decided I'd had enough. Time to retreat.

Otis had abandoned his post at the window and moved down the hallway with a dark-haired man with almond-shaped eyes. The way they had their heads bent together made me think they were in serious discussion. Probably over poor Polly.

Gertrude Hermann appeared. "Dr. Kwan. They're

trying to page you." She glanced in my direction. I pulled the door to the gym shut real fast.

"We're not allowed in there after hours," she informed me.

"I know that," I answered. She must not know about Polly. Unless she was a good actress.

Dr. Kwan grabbed his pager, looked at it, then back at Gertrude. "What's the problem?"

Gertrude enjoyed being the center of attention, that's for sure. She looked at me as she both answered the question and gave me the news. "Your husband is worried about his momma. Thomas and I got back from our walk, and I went over to introduce myself, and she was a little weird acting."

Dr. Kwan and I hustled toward the elevators, Gertrude two steps behind, while Otis returned to his office. As we neared the elevators, a gust of air hit us. Dr. Kwan and I turned to see the front doors open, two uniformed policemen entering.

Gertrude veered their direction. "Can I help you?" she boomed.

One of the ladies manning the front desk shot Gertrude a sour look and introduced herself to the police. Before I could overhear any more, the elevator doors popped open, inviting Dr. Kwan and me inside. Though I chafed at the idea of Gertrude getting an earful before I could, if something was wrong with Momma, I needed to know, and Hardy would need me.

A peek at Dr. Kwan revealed his eyes hard on those police fellows. "You had a chance to examine Polly yet?" I asked.

"Yes. Yes, I have. It was a terrible accident, Mrs. Barnhart. Tragic."

6

Turns out Momma's sugar was elevated. Dr. Kwan's visit was brief. Hardy had taken up residence next to his mother, her feet in his lap, her head nestled on her pillow. I saw the concern in his cocoa eyes.

"Tell him to stop fussing, LaTisha. I'm fine."

That's like telling a hummingbird to stop fluttering. Hardy loved his momma hard, which is just as it should be.

"Why don't you let him fuss, Momma. You'll miss him soon enough."

Her eyes latched onto Hardy and softened. "Suppose you're right."

"You feeling better now?" I asked.

"Wore out. Worn down. Nothing some sleep won't cure."

"If you're hungry, I can fix something light. Grilled chicken? A small salad?" I knew a thing or two about how to cook for her since she'd lived with us as she recovered from her stroke.

Hardy perked up at the sound of food and smacked his lips. "Sounds good to me. You already went to the store?"

"No, brought a few things along. I'll go in the morning." It didn't take any time to throw together the food for Hardy and me. He inhaled his and even got Matilda to eat a few bites.

I left them so I could try and find Sue Mie and talk to the cooks or a nurse. Someone. I couldn't imagine that they'd feed a resident something not part of her diet and wanted to be good and sure of their methods before leaving Momma in their hands. All this was making me think Hardy and me should have been more careful about screening assisted-living places. I admit, we chose the place more for its close location to Maple Gap than for any stellar reports of its care. And all this gave me an excuse to ask questions of the cafeteria lady Otis said could verify his alibi.

When I made it down to the main floor's common area, a small knot of the elderly ringed Gertrude.

". . .I don't know the facts yet, Lester," she was saying. "They had to wait for a while until someone found Mr. Payne. The police are with Mr. Payne now. All I know is that Polly is dead."

"She was okay this afternoon," one little lady said.

"Hopping mad about that new resident getting her apartment," another answered.

"Well, girls," Gertrude tried to placate, "all I can say is, all that doesn't matter now. She's gone."

Seems to me she should be shedding some salt right about now. On the other hand, with her and Polly spatting over Thomas, I guess they weren't friends. But shouldn't Gertrude at least have some remorse in her voice?

"It's gotta be the food here. That alone could kill anyone."

"It's not so bad, Charlie. You're just hard to please," Gertrude said.

I slipped down the hallway and poked my head into the cafeteria. Preparations for the evening meal would be in full swing, which meant the likelihood of talking to any kitchen worker was a big, fat zero.

Some sixth sense pulled me farther down that hall and toward Otis's office. The hallway door to his office was open, meaning I didn't have to duel with Miss Pillsbury.

Instead, I heard a new voice coming from Otis's domain. Female. Giggling laughter that conjured an image of blond hair. I expected to see a teenager, but the angle of the room prevented me from seeing more than two knees jutting into view. Very shapely knees. The voice fell to a whispery purr, and because of the one-sided responses, I figured this little lady was on the phone.

"That's *not* what I meant, and you know it. I've never seen anyone more capable than you."

An instinct deep in my gut told me not to bolt into the room and announce my presence. So I listened. Shamelessly. A list of possible identities filtered through my head. She could be Otis's wife, daughter, the daughter of a resident, the wife of the son of a resident, and on and on—the possibilities rolled like credits on a screen.

The purr shifted to a staccato forte. "I told you I have to have time to decide. It's not as easy as you might think. I'll talk to you about it later, okay?"

She did an air kiss into the phone.

I chose that moment to make my grand entrance. The woman sat in one corner of the sofa, pursing her lipsticked mouth as she stared into the mirror of her compact. Blond hair with dark roots. Uh-huh. Lookswise, she wasn't too bad. . .for what I'd guess to be a forty-year-old woman.

She snapped her compact shut and slid it and her cell phone into her purse. Her eyes raked over me like a lion sizing up its prey. Remind me not to get on her bad side.

"Are you the maid?" she asked.

Um-um-um. She was already on my bad side. "My name is LaTisha Barnhart. My mother-in-law is a resident here."

She had the grace to look ruffled by that announcement and tried to coo herself back into my good graces.

"You just look so strong and capable that I thought you must be one of the women who help lift the residents and clean up after them."

"My momma's been here less than twenty-four hours, and I've already been thinking we made a bad choice."

She flinched, crossed her legs, and started sing-songing in a tone that dripped sunshine and flowers. "Bridgeton Towers is a friendly community. I'm sure the residents will welcome your mother."

"It's not the residents that are the problem."

She flinched again, and glory be, was that a flush staining her cheeks? I enjoy helping people get in touch with their consciences, but it was time to go easy. I glanced at her left hand, saw the huge rock there, and decided to make a guess at who she was waiting for. "You here to see your husband? I believe he's talking with the police."

Her eyes went wide. "Otis is. . .I thought I saw a cruiser out front." She twisted and plunged her hand into her purse. "I just talked to him a few minutes ago."

More like an hour ago, but I wasn't going to say that. Maybe she'd called since then. "He's having a bad day."

She tugged out a tiny cell phone and pressed a button that beeped a reply. The keypad glowed blue. "Poor Oatsey. He hasn't left any messages."

Oatsey? Where could I go to throw up? Who did she think she was kidding? "One of the residents died. Polly Dent was her name."

"Oh." She dropped her phone back into her handbag. "Happens all the time with these old people."

So she knew about Polly? Or was that a blanket statement? Her crassness didn't make me like her more. This woman needed to be shook so hard saliva would fly from her mouth. I appointed myself the one to do it. "I'm sure it does, but when murder is suspected, that puts a new slant on things."

Her crimson lips rounded. "Murder!"

Just the reaction I was looking for. "They're interviewing your husband right now. They'll interview several people before it's over with."

She grasped the strap of her purse, knuckles white, face to match. "Otis would never do such a thing."

More a question than a statement. How curious. "Some people are driven by things not easily seen with the human eye."

A little gasp slipped through her lips, as if someone had just pricked her with a needle. She jerked to her feet, gathered her purse, and made a mad dash out the door and down the hall—toward the main entrance. You would figure a loving wife would rush to her husband's side and vow his innocence. Maybe it was time to look into Otis's alibi.

I stuck my head into the cafeteria on my way back down the hall. Even if I couldn't talk to anyone now, I hoped to catch a member of staff or someone who could answer my question about how the food for diabetics was prepared.

Nothing.

I did notice a separate room off the dining area. One I hadn't spotted before. But this time, the lights on inside and the presence of blue uniforms helped draw my attention real quick-like. The table in the center of this room was crowded with two police officers, Dr. Kwan, a woman dressed like a nurse, and Otis Payne.

7

About two hours later, at the request of an officer, I escorted my quaking husband down to the cafeteria for his grand inquisition. The smell of the roast beef from the evening meal still lingered. I tightened my arm around his shoulders. Poor sweet stuff. I knew how it felt to have the finger of accusation pointed in your direction. Come to think of it, Hardy's the one who got that finger crooked my direction after I found Marion Peters. I almost stopped right there in the hallway and told him he had this coming for what he'd done to me when I found Marion performing the horizontal stiff. Hardy's nervous shiver stilled my tongue before it could wag, so instead of giving a verbal assault, I pulled Hardy closer and rubbed the top of his grizzled hair. "Everything will be fine. You just go in there and tell the truth."

The officers had moved out of the banquet room and now commandeered two tables in the empty dining area. Officer Harvey Rhinehald introduced himself and the officer at the next table over. Officer Dwight Eldridge sent Hardy and me a simple nod in the way of greeting. While Rhinehald's rangy build and smooth skin didn't inspire much in the way of presence, he had a nice voice. He gave Hardy a good old boy grin. "Just a few questions, Mr. Barnhart."

Hardy didn't look convinced. As he sat, I took up a position right in back of him and laid my hand on my man's shoulder, offering my silent support, before putting some distance between us and giving them the privacy they required for questioning. Of course, I didn't move far enough away I couldn't hear when I strained real hard.

"Now, Mr. Barnhart, Mr. Payne. . .you'd seen Mrs. Dent at one point. . . I understand that Mrs. Dent had an issue with. . . Is that correct?"

Hardy nodded. "Yes, sir."

"Your mother. . .here?"

Another nod.

I humped my chair away from the table a couple of feet and dragged another chair closer so I could prop my feet up a bit before pressing back hard against the chair and cocking my head toward the conversation again.

We hadn't the chance to talk about it, but I wondered if Hardy was doing some heavy second-guessing about the safety of having Momma at Bridgeton Towers, like I was. We'd have to discuss it, and soon.

I caught most of the officer's next question. ". . .to me how Mrs. Dent reacted to your mother moving in?"

"She was really uptight. Said it was her apartment. That Mr. Payne had promised it to her. I went down to ask Mr. Payne about that later on, and he assured me that Mrs. Dent was wrong, that her name wasn't even on the list. . . ."

On and on the Q&A session went. Nothing new came out that I could latch onto. Hardy held up better than I thought he would. Innocence will do that.

I had more of a mind to pay attention to the table next to us when I saw Gertrude Hermann settling herself there. The officer gave her a warm smile and said something I couldn't hear, which irritated me. Gertrude, on the other hand, came across loud and clear.

"I wanted to tell you that Polly Dent was my friend. We didn't agree on everything, but she was a good soul."

The officer consulted his notes.

"She doesn't have any family," Gertie continued. "She and her ex-husband divorced years ago. He died this past summer."

Someone banged on the doors to the cafeteria. "Gertie! Gertie, you in there?"

Officer Eldridge's smile seemed a bit tight as he granted Gertrude permission to answer the door.

Another bang and Gertrude lurched to her feet. "Hold on, Mitzi, I'm coming."

Mitzi didn't seem to know quite what to do at the sight of so few people in the cafeteria or the two uniforms present. Her eyes did appear more alert than during the solitaire game, but with dementia, who knew?

Gertrude sat back down, leaving Mitzi by the double doors to continue gawking at us.

Officers Rhinehald and Eldridge exchanged a look I couldn't decipher. Rhinehald dismissed Mitzi's presence and locked eyes with Hardy again. "Mr. Barnhart, do you have any reason to believe Mrs. Dent was not acting in a normal fashion?"

Hardy turned his hands palm up. "How would I know? I just met her this morning."

Officer Rhinehald nodded and jotted something on the paper in front of him. "You're free to go, Mr. Barnhart."

Hardy bolted up out of that chair like he'd rubbed

a splinter in his tail, belying the calmness I thought he had possessed during the questioning. Funny how after all this time together, he could still surprise me.

From the other table, Gertrude's voice intruded on my thoughts. "Did you ask Mr. Payne about Sue Mie's uncle?"

Drat it that I couldn't hear the officer's response. No matter how hard I strained, Eldridge's voice didn't register. Something else happened in that second. Gertrude slid a glance over at me. Not just any kind of glance either. Believe me when I tell you I knew that look. I'd seen it umpteen times on the faces of my daughters as they savored some silly adolescent secret.

Hardy tugged on my hand. I gripped his hard and cut my eyes to him, hoping he'd tune in to the conversation and overhear something I couldn't. Maybe it was time for me to get my hearing checked.

Mitzi's walker clattered as she pointed herself in my direction, her feeble little body struggling behind the weight of the walker. What happened to the healthy, walkerless body she had earlier? I wondered if she'd spout off that crazy poetry again.

This time, though, she got so close to us I could smell garlic on her breath. She motioned us to lean in tight. "Not too nice. Little sugar, mostly spice. Since the death of mouse, a few months later and there goes her spouse."

8

I lay awake most of the night, bothered by Mitzi's latest poem. Was the woman simply entertaining herself with her little snippets of rhyme, or did they mean something? I had to make time and research dementia. What I needed was my house, my desk, my computer, the Internet. In that order. Hardy wanted to see his mother settled in before we went back home, which worked for us since she had a second bedroom, but I was getting antsy.

I finally decided sleep was not going to happen, so I shoved myself upright, letting my legs dangle over the edge of the bed. Hardy didn't stir. He slept like a dead man after we'd talked about saying he'd only seen Polly before dinner.

I checked on Momma, who also slept soundly, and went to her little kitchen area to rattle around for a cup. Minus my regular mocha mix, I'd have to settle for second best—warm milk. Problem. Momma didn't have any milk in her refrigerator. Harsh reality settled on me in an instant. I was in an apartment with almost no food in the refrigerator and only a handful of sugar-free snacks. How did people live like this?

Is this what I had to look forward to? I think I'd go crazy without a kitchen full of staples ready to be baked up at a moment's notice. If I get a hankering for something, I make it. Simple. But not stuck in a place like this where everything was regimented. I closed my eyes, sadder than I'd been for a long time.

Looked like I'd be drinking water—cold or hot—at least I had that choice. I chose to sip warm water, satisfying my throat-aching thirst, jotting a list of the things I'd have to pick up at the store in the morning. Matilda loved her tea and would probably want a cup if she held true to the routine she'd developed while staying with Hardy and me during her recovery.

Those first few months, I'd cooled it with a splash of milk and watched as it spilled down her stroke-slackened mouth. Over time, she'd grown stronger, recovering some of her muscle control. It had been a terrible time for Hardy and me both. Mainly because it brought the whole I'm-getting-older thing into tight focus.

How would it feel to be a resident at an assisted-living facility? To know the place you called home on earth was penultimate to your final destination?

I closed my eyes and leaned into the comfort of the recliner, pressing the warm mug to my lips. Waves of despair, brutal and sharp in their force, washed over me, not for myself but for the Pollys and Matildas, the Gertrudes and Mitzis.

Stark in its oppressiveness, a thought jolted me. Suicide. Could Polly, irritated and disappointed after Mr. Payne's news, have committed suicide? On a treadmill? The absurdity of the idea made me grin. *La Tisha, honey, you'd better get a grip on yourself, thinking fool thoughts about little old women and treadmills of death.*

Wide awake now, curiosity at full sail, I slipped into my clothes and palmed my room key. The hallways were wide and white, and an oak banister ran the length of each side, about wrist height. I sucked air into my lungs in a rhythmic breathing that never failed to relax me, picturing the tension easing with each exhalation.

On the main floor common area, a TV blared a rerun to its audience of empty chairs and stark walls, and one lone woman slumped in an oversized armchair. As if my breathing somehow interrupted her sleep pattern, she snuffled awake, strange pale eyes staring a hole right through me.

"Good morning, Miss Mitzi," I whispered.

Her solemn expression faded to a smile. "Couldn't sleep while counting sheep?"

A little of this rhyming stuff went a long way. If I had to listen to Mitzi all day, I just might need a nice, softly padded cell. "It's a strange place. My mind won't adjust and settle down." I choked on my poor choice of words. Like telling someone you didn't approve of the atmosphere of her home. "I thought hoofing myself around the building might help me get to sleep."

She tilted her head from side to side. "Did you take the time to think on my rhyme?"

Dr. Seuss, meet your match. "I have. Can you tell me what you mean? Does 'A dark shadow at the door' mean something or someone?"

Mitzi's smile widened, her eyes sparkled. "Someone."

I waited for her to explain, but she seemed to enjoy stumping me. "So what you're saying, the poems, they're riddles?"

"Riddles, rhymes, taking up time. Mom used to say that. Mixed-up words that made no sense." She pressed her palms together. I watched as her expression became distant, as if she'd slipped from her surroundings to an area of pure delight. Joy wept from her expression, giving birth to two fat tears.

I'd lost her somehow. My throat swelled as I watched her cover her face and sob over some undefined sorrow. *God in Your mercy, comfort her heart.* I don't know how Hardy would ever survive this if his mother went this route. His tender heart would shatter, for sure.

After a while, Mitzi's hands fell to her lap. Quietly, slowly, I reached out to touch her hand. She lifted her head, and I saw the blankness of her stare, her hand stark white against my black skin. She squeezed real tight. As if I were her grip on reality.

When Hardy finally rattled his bones from bed, I'd already gone to the grocery store and back and had hot water waiting for his mother, and a poached egg, toast, and hash browns for Hardy. He dug in with a vengeance.

"Eat that up before Momma comes out, or she'll want to eat it, too. We've got to get her used to going to the cafeteria." I whispered all that, then I sprayed Lysol in the air for the second time to do away with the smells of home cooking. We could have eaten downstairs, but the meals weren't cheap for nonresidents.

Hardy ate like a vacuum. Slugged back his juice like a man caught in the desert sun and belched loud enough to cause his mother to holler at him from the other room.

"I taught you manners, boy, don't be forgettin' them. What you all cooking in there anyway?" She appeared in the doorway, nose pointed at the ceiling.

"And whatever you're spraying isn't working, LaTisha. Hash browns, poached eggs, and toast."

Hardy gave me a wry grin. "You gotta admit, she's good."

I planted my hands on my hips. "Bet you can't tell me what kind of toast."

Matilda pulled up beside me at the sink and raised one eyebrow. "Wheat toast this morning, though you normally buy five-grain. Now"—she pivoted on her heel—"I'm heading down to get my breakfast."

When she shut the door, Hardy started cackling like a hyena. "I never thought I'd see the day when LaTisha Barnhart met her match, but I guess Momma's the one."

I huffed at him. "You get in that bathroom and put a shine on your tooth."

He went, laughing the whole way.

I was anxious to go downstairs and find out what the police had concluded about Polly's fall, suspecting they had determined it was an accident.

"Hurry up!" I yelled after Hardy. Every time I wanted to hotfoot it somewhere, it seemed like he shifted into low gear. I missed my broomstick. Back home we had a system. I had a broomstick standing by the hall table on the first floor. Whenever Hardy ran late, I'd use it to tap on the ceiling to let him know he was taking too long. It annoys him no end when I do that, 'cause, you see, *I* don't have to patch the holes in the ceiling.

Thinking about home made me wish I could stir up a batch of pot stickers—my newest yummy treat. Maybe a nice batch of spice cookies and a deep-dish lasagna. Cooking always helps me think, and I sorely needed some good thinking time.

"You got that look in your eye," Hardy observed, smacking his lips and blowing his fresh toothpasty breath on me. "Can't resist me now, can you?"

What had gotten into this boy? "Sure I can. Now let's get."

He pouted all the way down the hall. When we got on the elevator, I could see his pooched lip. Poor man. I coiled my arm around his shoulders and pulled him close, landing a kiss on his lips. "There now. You taste as sweet as chocolate."

"As good as Gerard's Belli?"

It took me a minute. "You mean Ghirardelli."

His eyes sparkled. "I thought it was mighty funny to name a chocolate after someone's gut."

When we finally made it off the elevator, I was surprised to find Otis Payne sitting beside Thomas Philcher and Gertrude. Wasn't Sunday a day off anymore? Maybe Polly's fall meant writing out more reports and such, and Sunday was the day to do it.

Thomas looked forlorn. He'd probably heard the news of Polly's demise only this morning. Beside him, Gertrude sat, unusually quiet, even kind of sad looking.

"Missing Polly?" I asked the group, though I was looking at Gertrude.

"I can hardly believe she's gone," Gertrude whispered. Her agonized tone spoke volumes. Interesting, she hadn't seemed so down about it when Thomas wasn't there last evening. Maybe she was depressed because he was so obviously saddened by the news.

Thomas continued to stare at the gnarled head of his simple wooden cane.

"The police didn't stay long last night," Otis offered, his eyes hard on me. "After talking to everyone, they ruled it an accident and said there was no further need for investigation."

"I'm sure your wife will be relieved to hear that."

Otis looked surprised. "My wife?"

"She was here yesterday to visit you. When I told her what had happened, she seemed distressed."

"Why, yes, of course." He cleared his throat. "She is easily upset by such things. A tender spirit, you might say."

I might not say that. If she'd talked to him, she sure hadn't mentioned dropping by. I tried to rein in my suspicious mind by telling myself it was possible they hadn't talked much the night before. Everyone seemed relieved at the news of the police declaring Polly's death an accident. There would be no investigation. I could finish getting Momma settled and go home.

Otis got to his feet real sudden-like. "I have some work to do, Thomas." He clapped a hand on the other man's shoulder. "Hang in there."

Mitzi's strange poem came back to me.

A dark shadow at the door. Polly Dent on the floor. Not everyone plays fair. Life for him is solitaire. She'd said it meant someone. If only she weren't sick. The other rhyme floated through my brain. *Not too nice. Little sugar, mostly spice. Since the death of mouse, a few months later and there goes her spouse.*

Mindless ramblings. Gertrude would know about Mitzi's state of mind. "How's Mitzi this morning? I found her asleep in this chair late last night."

"She creeps around here most nights. Drives me crazy. We used to room together, but I'm a light sleeper, so it didn't work out."

"Does she always rhyme everything like that?"

Gertie's smile was genuine. "She sure does. She taught at the University of Colorado. Loved poetry, even as a child. She self-published a couple books of her poems." She laughed. "She has this thing—used to drive me crazy, but I'm used to it now—where she'd meet people then kind of invent rhymes describing their personalities or something about them."

"Really?" My heart slapped up against my ribs. This must be important. Had to be. "How long has she been doing it?"

Gertrude looked to Thomas. He answered, "Ever since I've been here. I got here before Gertrude. Mitzi's been here longest." Thomas tapped his cane against the floor and guffawed. "She's the one who first dared to call that foreign fellow 'rat face.' She kind of rhymed it. Everyone got it but him."

"Chao was his name," Gertrude mumbled. "Sue Mie's uncle. Don't you remember, Thomas?"

Thomas's smile was beatific. This guy oozed charm.

"Does he still live here?" I asked.

Gertrude warmed to the subject. "Nah. He fell over dead in the hallway, had everyone scared. Thought for sure someone else would die of a heart attack. Mitzi went around for weeks afterward repeating some silly poem about a mouse no longer in the house."

My blood ran cold in my veins. *Mouse. . .since the death of mouse, a few months later and there goes the spouse.*

I holed up in the room all morning working to decipher those poems. Gertrude had divulged far more than she knew. I explained about Mitzi's poems to Hardy as he gummed up his sandwich, brow creased in think mode.

"Mitzi's old, LaTisha. Probably just making stuff up to keep you jumping." Hardy snapped open the local paper I'd bought on my trip to the grocery store, as if his declaration ended the debate.

"But why?"

A grunt was the only reply I received. He turned the page, hand groping for the sandwich plate, finding it, then disappearing behind the paper again. The sandwich returned to the plate another bite smaller.

"Hardy. Put down that paper and look at me."

"Please, LaTisha, I'm eating."

Very funny. I could just imagine his smug smirk over his little jibe. "You're gonna be sucking your food through a straw if you don't talk to me."

He bent back a corner of the paper, enough to make eye contact. "Are you threatening me, Mrs. Barnhart?"

"I don't make threats—I make promises."

His eyes glittered. "After seven babies, you should know I'm a lover not a fighter." He eyed my plate. "Why aren't you eating?"

Even when I made the sandwich, the idea of eating it hadn't appealed to me. I sipped at my glass of water instead. "I need to talk, and you need to listen to me."

He frowned but folded the paper and put it aside.

"Gertrude said Mitzi enjoys poetry. Then Gertrude says Mitzi often makes up these rhymes about people and that she creeps around the building at night. What if the poems she said to me mean something? What if she saw something?"

"You're really reaching."

"I can see motives in some of these people."

Hardy rubbed the rim of his plate. "I don't."

"Otis Payne's wife acted real strange the other day. Did you know she'd come by to visit her husband? But she hotfooted after I told her he was being questioned by the police about Polly's fall." Even as I spoke, I realized what Hardy said was true. I didn't have one solid motive. I kept talking anyway. "And why was Polly in that exercise room after hours?"

Hardy pushed aside the empty lunch plate, licked his finger, rolled it in the bread crumbs, and popped it into his mouth. "Best to let it go, LaTisha. I think finding Marion has made you think murder is behind every dead body."

I didn't want Hardy to be right. I really didn't. Though the investigation had about killed me, solving Marion's murder was the most satisfying thing I'd done since watching my youngest graduate from high school.

What I needed to do was get out and talk to people. Do some digging.

"If Polly lived here a long time, she probably knew a lot about the other residents." This from Hardy, Mr. You-Don't-Have-a-Motive. "Could be worth bending some ears over."

"Whistling a different song now."

"No. But figuring out those poems would be like solving a minimystery."

A diversion. He saw them only as a way to satisfy my curiosity. "This isn't sudoku," I huffed.

Hardy leaned back in his chair. "What's the first line?"

"A dark shadow at the door."

"Is that literal? Dark, meaning skin color? Or did she really only see a shadow?"

"You think she saw you there when you talked to Polly?"

He shrugged. "Could of. I didn't see anyone in the hallway, but I also wasn't paying attention. But what *door* is she talking about?"

"The next line is 'Polly Dent on the floor,' which makes me think it's the door to the exercise room."

"Could be." Hardy's hand rasped down his cheek. "But what if she saw Polly somewhere else on the floor? You're assuming she saw her dead in the exercise room."

"Yeah, but why would she think it's so important to tell me this thing if she didn't think there was something strange going on?"

"Early dementia, LaTisha. You can't forget that part."

He didn't believe any of it. I could tell, and for the first time, doubt scratched at my brain. "What do you know about dementia?"

"Alzheimer's is the most common form of dementia and affects the cells in the brain, causing them to deteriorate at a higher rate than cells of those not having the condition. Some of the symptoms include forgetfulness, usually accompanied with confusion and difficulties retaining knowledge of function, such as cooking. Patients will not only forget the pot on the stove but that they were even cooking. Inability to recognize numbers or do simple math. Spatial and temporal orientation problems, personality changes, mood swings, and language problems."

I was impressed. "And how do you know all that?"

He flashed his tooth in an affable grin. "Read a pamphlet on it yesterday."

"Here I thought you were digging and finally struck genius."

He winked. "Did that a long time ago when I married you."

"I hear you sugar talking me."

The light left his expression, and he leaned forward. "You feeling all right?"

"I'm fine."

"You look all wore out."

"I need to get back to my house." To my kitchen is what I really meant.

"Four, five more days, babe, and Momma should be settled in real good."

"You worried about her being here now that Polly had that fall? Gertrude also mentioned that Sue Mie— the nurse lady who you ran into yesterday—her uncle was here, and he fell. They think he had a heart attack after the hall railing pulled out from the wall." Asking him about Polly's fall reminded me that I had to look into what had been served in the cafeteria that could have led to Momma's sugar spiking. While I did that, I would check out Otis's alibi.

"Sometimes things happen like that." He did a little scratch along his nose. A significant scratch. Married to him for as long as I've been, this particular scratch was the one that told me he was struggling for composure. One of those little nervous giveaways that most people have, and once used to seeing their reactions, anyone close to them can see what they're thinking.

He had it in his head that his momma might meet a terrible death. I should probably explain something. You see, Hardy's mother is all he has. When he was four, his father left them. He's never felt a need to find his father, and his father apparently feels the same, but I know the deep-down hurt he's carried over being left like that.

I hitched my chair closer to him and pulled him into one of my hugs. He fit just perfect in the circle of my arms. This reminder of his vulnerability put my longing for home on the back burner. Hardy needed this, needed to know his momma was safe, happy, and content, which meant I needed to shelve my selfish need for home and honor him. It was that simple.

Hilda Broumhild gave new meaning to cooking. Think svelte brunette with enough curves to make a CURVES AHEAD sign envious. Hardy about dropped his last tooth, and I about helped him through the process when I saw his reaction.

"Someone should arrest her," he mumbled.

"Why?"

"'Cause she's gonna make some poor old man die of a heart attack."

"Good thing your heart is strong."

"It's not beat this hard in a long time."

Hilda was approaching head-on. I gave her a huge smile and hissed at Hardy. "It's not the only thing gonna be beat hard if you don't behave."

He slid me a mischievous smirk. "I'm married, not blind."

"Hello. I'm Hilda Broumhild. Is there a problem I can help you with?"

Got to hand it to her, her momma done raised her with pretty manners. "My mother-in-law moved in here yesterday. She ate here for the first time and experienced a spike in her sugar level. I'm wanting to know what you served."

She must have had these inquiries all the time from concerned family members. Without hesitation she motioned for us to follow her. "Last night we served roast beef and mashed potatoes and a slice of blueberry pie."

"Blueberry pie?"

Her smile revealed nice white grillwork. "The diabetics get the same thing but the sugar-free variety."

"Is there a possibility she could have been given a slice that was not sugar free?"

Hilda pushed through the double doors and into the commercial kitchen, complete with gleaming stainless steel countertops and appliances. She went straight to a wall where several clipboards hung in a row and took one down. "These have the names of patients and their dietary restrictions." Her finger slipped down the list. "There is only one new resident listed. Mrs. Matilda Barnhart?"

"That's my mother," Hardy confirmed.

"She is listed as diabetic and should have received a diabetic meal."

"How can we be certain?"

Hilda replaced her clipboard. "I don't serve the meals. . .is it Mrs. Barnhart?"

"Call me LaTisha, please."

Another flash of the grillwork. "We do our best to ensure the residents remain within their dietary guidelines."

"A mistake could happen."

Her smile wilted a bit. "There are many factors to consider. We often find that the residents buy food products they shouldn't, or their families bring them candy and such even though it's against policy. In spite of the fact that we have midafternoon and evening snacks, many of the residents either aren't aware of—or capable of—sticking to the foods best suited for their body's needs."

I'd definitely have to have another chat with Sue Mie. Maybe the snack she'd given me for Matilda wasn't the right one. Mistakes must be common. Certainly human but mistakes can cost lives, and I didn't want to be forgetting that either. As I tried to think of a way to bring up Otis Payne and his alibi, Hardy piped up and solved my problem.

"You heard about Polly Dent's death? It happened about the time Mr. Payne was taking his dinner hour in here."

Hilda's laugh sounded a bit too gay. Mental note made. "The girls and I were eating our dinner when Polly came in to get Mr. Payne. He'd just sat down. He told Polly she'd have to wait, but she insisted. He left for a while—"

"How long?"

Hilda's gaze skittered off to the left. "Probably five minutes. Then he came back and finished up his meal."

Oh, really? Doesn't sound like Otis, old boy, was completely honest with his so-called alibi. And he left *with* Polly. . . . My brain was heating up. A miscommunication or something more?

Hardy and I exchanged a look. The slick feel of victory was all mine. Maybe Mitzi had seen a thing or two. At worst, it meant nothing; at best, it meant foul play. Hardy's expression was best interpreted as a *Maybe I was wrong after all.* If my girdle hadn't been so tight, I might have done a victory shimmy.

Hardy grabbed my hand on our way out. "Did I tell you you're the smartest, cutest lady I know?"

"I was beginning to wonder if you remembered."

"Never forgot it. Not once since the day we united in holy deadlock."

I hauled him into another hug, and we laughed

ourselves silly. When we settled ourselves down, I sent him back upstairs to check on his momma and ventured off on my own to find a familiar face. I had me a whole list of people who I needed to talk to.

I didn't recognize anyone in the common area, and Mr. Payne's office was empty. Dinnertime would be a good opportunity to talk to other residents. No doubt they'd all come out for that event. The area where I had encountered Mitzi showed no evidence of activity, except a deck of cards laid out, as if someone had interrupted her game of solitaire, and a few board games.

Life for him is solitaire.

Obviously a man. Probably someone Mitzi had known for quite a while to make such a judgment. Otis? Thomas? Maybe one of the residents I had never met. What would it mean for someone's life to be like the game solitaire? I rejected the most obvious reasoning. No way could it mean someone lonely. That explanation didn't feel right.

Not everyone plays fair. Life for him is solitaire.

Translation: Life was all about him. His wants. His needs. And he didn't play fair. That kind of selfishness could be found in every man I knew. Women, too. Unless they were full up with the Lord. He leaves no room for selfishness of any kind.

I puffed out a frustrated breath and began to prowl around the building. Instead of heading from Otis's office back toward the common area, I continued down the hallway past the exercise room, soon realizing the hallways wrapped around in a huge octagon.

The hallway ended at double doors. A keypad indicated this must be the nursing section of Bridgeton

Towers, where residents live who require higher levels of care. A few nurses were clearly visible, but I knew I wasn't getting into that section—no way, no how.

I retraced my steps, noticing a hallway just before the exercise room, and turned into it, surprised to find an elevator straight ahead, a large room off to my left, and a door on the right, adjacent to the elevator.

I stabbed at the button on the elevator a few times. It was locked. Probably a service elevator. The other door was locked, too. It would have led somewhere behind the exercise room was my best guess.

The other door opened into a large room, where the scent of fabric softener and the hum of machines clued me in to what the room was used for. A home wouldn't be a home if there wasn't dirty laundry to be done.

I heard a dryer door being opened, and the hum stopped. I pushed the door wider to get a better look inside. A middle-aged man stood in front of the dryer, pulling out clothes and tossing them onto a nearby table. He left the door open a crack and started sorting his white clothes. I noticed his gnarled and bent hands as he struggled to fold a T-shirt.

"Hello there," I greeted.

His head snapped up. "Hi," he responded, returning his attention to the T-shirt.

This boy was as shy as my Shakespeare.

I advanced a step and debated whether to offer my help. Despite his disability, he seemed fully capable of taking care of himself, and I didn't want to offend that sense of self-reliance. I aimed for something basic. I beamed my brightest. "I'm touring around trying to figure out where everything is. My mother-in-law just moved in."

His lopsided grin came slow but was warm and welcoming. "I saw you moving her stuff in yesterday. I'm across the hall. Name's Darren."

Ah. It clicked then. *The door peeker.*

"You been here a long time, Darren?"

His hand tremored, spilling the top T-shirt he was folding into a heap. He stared down at the jumble and blew out a breath. "It takes me a little longer to get things folded sometimes." He picked up the shirt, shook it out, and began again.

"I had seven children. Folding became a specialty of mine, if you want some help."

"Been here seven years," he offered.

"Mr. Payne seems like a good director."

He finally got the T-shirt wrestled into form and started on another. I suspected his nonanswer to my offer of help was his way of saying "Thanks but I'm capable." His nonanswer on Mr. Payne just made me plain curious. "I've met Gertrude Hermann, Thomas Philcher, and Mitzi Mullins. Polly Dent, too."

He'd tackled another T-shirt by then and added it to his pile. "It's really sad about Polly. Some people didn't like her."

"Did you?"

He shrugged. "Gertrude didn't like her much."

"What can you tell me about Mitzi Mullins. Has she been here a long time?"

His head bobbed, and the lopsided smile slid back into place. And something else I couldn't quite finger right then.

"She used to live down the hall from me. We'd get

together and play cards. Since I'm so shaky, she made this thing for me to set my cards in." He lowered his face, and I sensed some form of despair as his expression wilted. "But she moved to a different hallway since she's been having a harder time concentrating."

My heart smiled at his choice of words. What a kind way to say it. I knew, too, that he missed her company, and I wondered if anyone bothered to visit him to play cards anymore. I'd have to introduce him to Matilda. They'd be quite the pair.

"Did you know Polly Dent?"

His hand tremored, and his face pulled into a frown. "Everyone knew her. She always talked real loud to me."

"She talked loud to us, too, so don't feel bad. Maybe she was hard of hearing. My mother-in-law sometimes ignores people, but her hearing is fine."

His answer could have been a sigh; it was such a soft "Yeah."

Silence reigned supreme as I watched him fold another T-shirt, sensing both awkwardness and something else. Something harder to define. "Why don't you come by this evening, and I'll introduce you to my husband and mother-in-law. We can even play a few games down in the common area."

He pulled another T-shirt from his pile, flexing his fingers as if to dispel pain. "Are you going to come see her?"

"You mean my mother-in-law?"

He nodded.

"She's family. Families take care of each other."

Another whispery sigh. "It can get lonely here."

"Do you have relatives to come see you?"

His hands stilled, his head wagging in the negative.

My heart ached for him. "Since my husband, Hardy, and me don't live far away and we're both retired, we'll probably come at least twice a week, maybe more."

Darren fisted one gnarled hand, staring at it as if seeing it for the first time. "Would you—would you come by and visit me?"

I couldn't help it. The way he said it wrenched me so bad, I had to do some loving on him. I opened my arms and gathered this man, little more than a stranger, into my arms, sharing the pain of his isolation if only for a short time. "We'd be glad to, honey."

At first his response was what I'd expect, stiff and scared, but I held on until his arms crept around me in a sudden, fierce embrace before I let him go.

"And you have a standing invitation to share the holiday meals with us at our house. We'll come and take Momma and you home with us. How does that sound?"

His eyes, long-lashed and brown, lit with a ray of pure sunshine. "Really?"

"Yup. I make a mean turkey, and my pumpkin pie can't be beat. If my kids come home, you'll have to hustle to the table or you'll be licking crumbs."

"I've never had a real family."

"Well, we'll consider you the white sheep of ours."

His eyes went wide until he realized I was teasing, then laughter bubbled up and sprinkled out in little giggles.

It always amazes me how a true friend can march into our lives so quickly, if we're just willing to be friendly first. I flicked my hand to indicate the room. "Are you the laundryman?"

He patted a shirt flat with his stiff fingers and tugged another wrinkled one from the mass. Instead of waiting any longer, I stretched across the table and heaved the pile closer, then I plucked up a piece out of the pile. It turned out to be a pair of shorts. My eyes darted to Darren's. His face flushed scarlet.

"None of that, now. I raised five boys. Shorts happened every wash day. When they got old enough to do their own laundry and the piles got high in their room, I'd do it for them. But they sure paid a steep price." I laughed outright at the memory. "I'd throw something red into their load. Never seen boys so eager to do their own laundry after that. Worked every time. Five times over." I quick folded the shorts I held and pulled another pair from the pile as Darren finished his shirt.

We worked in silence a bit before I finally remembered to ask, "What's the elevator for?"

"Linens get taken up and down that way. Only the laundry lady and the nurses have a key."

"How about this room? The residents come in here to do their laundry?"

He shrugged. "Yeah."

Okay, so this didn't seem to mean much to my investigation. Still, I'd tuck away the information. One never knew.

I chatted Darren up, asking about his parents—divorced and estranged from him. No brothers and sisters either, which explained why he didn't have anyone come see him. I helped him finish the pile of clothes, reminded him about my invitation for later this evening, and left.

I jabbed at the button of the elevator one more time before recollecting that Darren'd said the nurses and maintenance people used a key to operate it. I wondered if anyone else used it. Placed as it was near the offices, it made sense the director and other employees might make use of it. At least sometimes.

I took the main elevator up to the second floor again and mentally calculated the service elevator's position to be. . .right. . .about. . .here.

Problem was, there was a room there that looked to be used for storage. The elevator must let off inside. Double, solid white doors and a huge lock shouted *dead end* in my head, followed by the rhyming words of a now familiar singsong voice. . .

"Darkened hands, pulling, tugging. . ."

I turned, recognizing Mitzi. She stared at the white doors, continuing her latest rhyme.

"Into the secret room. Like snow in the palm of the hand, in the end it sealed her doom."

"Mitzi, you about sent this black woman to the floor." She didn't have her walker. No wonder I didn't hear her coming. Come to think of it, I hadn't seen the walker last night either.

Her gaze held mine for a second, then it transferred to the locked doors again. She repeated her ditty then tacked on the first one. "A dark shadow at the door. Polly Dent on the floor. . ."

"You see someone go in here, Mitzi? Is that what you're trying to tell me?" Frustration tightened my voice and made it louder than the gentle tone I wanted to use.

Her eyes slid back to me. My back tingled as I watched her gaze go from unfocused to razor sharp. "Don't let them get away with it, Mrs. Barnhart."

If I spooked easy, I'd have turned tail and beat it in a hot second. But the window of her clarity could close any second, and I needed to get a hand up before it slammed. "Who, Mitzi?"

"Ask Sue Mie about mouse."

Not *the* mouse, just *mouse*. Before I could squeeze in another question, Mitzi scurried off with more speed than someone who used a walker should be capable of.

11

I spent the afternoon hours with a pencil and paper, continuing to dissect Mitzi's poems and the possibilities they stirred in my brain. Within an hour, I had several ideas and a very capable assistant.

"The solitaire thing reminds me of Bryton. Remember as a young'un when he hated playing with the other kids because they always won?" Momma pursed her lips and scratched her head. Nothing wrong with this woman's mind. "He started playing solitaire all the time after that."

Her memory brought it back to me. Bryton, my second son, is fiercely competitive. If he's not numero uno, watch out.

Matilda stabbed her long brown finger at the pad of paper I'd written the poems on. "You ask me, whoever this one's about is probably the culprit. Maybe he pushed her or tripped her or something."

I jotted down everything she suggested, trying to keep up with the flow of her words.

She squinted, a sure sign she was thinking hard. "'Mouse' sounds like a nickname, and obviously a married person, since 'There goes the spouse' says that."

I thought on that good and hard. Spouse. Mouse. Just the two words stuck together to make the thing rhyme? Was Mitzi in her right mind enough to be that good with poetry? Had she really seen something going on? "Mitzi has dementia. How you suppose she can rhyme so clearly?"

Momma snapped her fingers—or tried to snap her fingers. Arthritis does that. "Easy enough. You said she was a professor. If poetry is her love, it's probably what's going to stick hardest in her mind as she gets older. Don't you notice how we old folk go back in time as our bodies go forward?"

I nodded.

"Same kind of thing. She's used to expressing herself that way, so it comes natural."

"Any thoughts on the secret room?"

"You ever known me not to have an opinion?" A rhetorical question to be sure. Momma rubbed the polished head of her cane. I could hear her wheels whirring hard. No dead hamster on this wheel. She thumped her cane on the floor. "You need to get into that room. Something's in there."

Right. Just like that.

"This snow stuff is important, too. Mitzi's sayin' it sealed her doom."

"Something on her hands sealed her doom?"

Matilda raised her eyebrows at me. "Gloves? Might look like snow."

I thought hard on that. "She wasn't choked to death, and it says, 'In the palm of her hand.' "

"Still say you need to get in that room."

I'd have to figure something out. I could charm my way in. Ha! No, that's Hardy's territory. I doubted Otis would take me on a tour of the storage room. Someone else should have access to it, a janitor maybe. I'd have to keep my eyes wide open.

I flicked a hand over the poems and my notes. "You think Polly's fall wasn't an accident?" Initially we'd thought it best to keep Polly's fall from Momma, but I wanted her input. If she felt the least bit insecure about remaining at Bridgeton Towers, she'd let us know.

Momma Matilda's smile melted over me in a way that made me miss my mother and extra glad I had my mother-in-law. Her cool hand covered mine. "If anything terrible is happening around here, you'll find out, honey. I trust you."

"I don't think Hardy's convinced."

"What does that boy know? He fathered seven children, but, honey, you mothered 'em. And mothering is looking way beyond the outside of a body. The good momma sees inside the head and knows what makes her babies tick. They follow their intuition and act when they need to. There's no better momma than you, LaTisha. None."

"I have a great husband." A lame attempt at modesty.

Matilda saw through me like I was plastic wrap. "Hardy's my baby, and he's smart and talented, but it's the day-to-day that made your babies into solid, productive adults. You got a right to be proud, and the modesty stuff doesn't settle well on you."

If I ever wanted a bouquet of roses from my mother-in-law, I sure was getting it, and it was humbling and beautiful. Her words made me feel strong and loved. I'd savor this feeling for days to come.

Speaking of feeling loved. . . "I met a young man today. Darren's his name. Seems mighty lonely to me. Told him to meet us downstairs for some cards this evening. I'll introduce you."

Matilda pinned me with her eyes. "I'd love to meet the boy."

12

Matilda and me sat in companionable silence for a long time. She seemed far away, and I didn't want to disturb her none, so I glued my eyes to the paper of Mitzi's poems. Shadows, hands, snow. . .it all whirled in my head something powerful. I heaved a sigh and decided I needed some noise. How I ached to cook, but talk would have to fill the spot since I was a long way from my kitchen.

"I met another one of your neighbors today, Momma."

Matilda tipped her head at me. "You mean that fine-looking fellow. Thomas something-or-other?"

"You met him?"

"He and that Gertrude woman introduced themselves at lunchtime. She said she'd tried the day before, but I was having my sugar problem and probably didn't remember her. I can tell you I recognized his smell though."

I wondered if I'd heard right and even stuck my finger in my ear and gave it a good wringing. "You recognized how he smelled?"

"Sure. It was strong. That's how I knew he was my neighbor before he ever said who he was. I was standing in front of his apartment the other day, remember? Saw that Polly woman making a mess inside. She hit the road when she saw me, but what I remembered most was the whole apartment smelled wrong. That's how I knew I wasn't in the right place, then Hardy came along and got me all straightened out."

"You trippin'." Stunned was an understatement. "You mean to tell me you saw Polly in Thomas's apartment the other day?" It would have been before Polly'd gone down to the exercise room.

"Well, I got in." She massaged her forehead as if doing so might help her recall specifics. "I think the door was unlocked. I'm a little foggy about all of it, but I remember that smell and seeing her."

Foggy I could understand, what with her sugar probably on the rise at that point. "Did she say anything to you? Explain herself?"

"She was pulling something out of a drawer. When she saw me standing there, she shoved right past me."

I leaned back in my chair and let it all sink in. "Why didn't you say something sooner?"

"With the move and everything, I really hadn't given it much thought. But if someone did Polly in, you might look into Thomas. I don't expect he was happy if he found out she was poking around his room."

So Thomas had seen Polly poking around in his apartment. It was a real good time to invite Thomas to sit with us during dinner so we could have us a little chat. Gertrude hadn't managed to make it down to the cafeteria in time to put her hooks in him, and I wanted the opportunity to smell him out for myself. Pun intended. Funny thing, I didn't smell much.

He greeted Momma with a shallow bow, giving me the same and extending his hand to Hardy as if eating at Bridgeton required fine manners. He even stood until Momma and I were seated. Hardy, on the other hand, planted his rump first thing.

I cleared my throat.

He lifted his head and hiked an eyebrow.

"Mr. Philcher has such fine manners," I dripped.

He wagged his bottom against the chair and grinned that insufferable grin of his. "I wanted to make sure the chairs were comfortable for you ladies before you sat down."

I frosted him with a look and lowered myself into the nicely cushioned, dark blue upholstered seat.

"So, Mr. Philcher," I began the conversation. I flicked open my napkin and spread it on my lap. Hardy flicked his open and tucked it into his shirt. I knew he was doing it to agitate me and chose to ignore his antics. "What can you tell us about this fine establishment?"

Matilda reached over and yanked out Hardy's paper ascot. *Go, Momma!*

Thomas smothered a grin and toyed with his water glass. "I find that Bridgeton Towers meets my needs, Mrs. Barnhart. I needed somewhere to go, and this was as good a place as any."

For a minute there, I thought he wasn't going to give me a straight answer. Come to think of it, maybe I didn't get one. "What did you do before coming here?"

Thomas sipped his water. "I worked as a waiter in a fine restaurant."

Could have fooled me. I expected him to say he'd been a butler or a tycoon in some big business.

"When the restaurant changed management after

twenty years, I decided it was time to ease out. Keeping up with the small lawn and such didn't interest me anymore either, so I moved in here."

"Never married?" Hardy asked.

"I never felt inclined to commit myself. I was on the move quite a bit in my youth." He sipped at his water and dabbed his mouth with the napkin. "I'm quite certain a woman would have tired of it quickly."

"Mrs. Hermann seems to enjoy your company," Momma offered.

"Gertrude complements my quiet nature."

This man's tongue practically dripped oil. "What do you think about Polly's accident?" I decided to crank the conversation into high gear when I glimpsed Gertrude entering the cafeteria. She was looking over the crowd, too, which meant it would only be a matter of time before. . .

"I'll miss Mrs. Dent. She was an interesting and dear companion," Thomas said.

"She was sure set on having Momma's room. Why you think she'd be so set on it?"

For the first time, I detected discomfort in his demeanor.

Gertrude was fast approaching.

The server arrived with Momma's plate, as well as Mr. Philcher's. I frowned down at the runny-looking mashed potatoes and hamburger patty. "What's this?"

"Salisbury steak." Thomas smiled. "Not quite the caliber of meal I'm used to but tasty nonetheless."

Gertrude was bearing down fast. Twenty feet. . .

I wiped my mouth as my stomach roiled in disgust. "I'm guessing Polly wanted the room to be close to you."

Fifteen feet.

"We were quite good friends." Thomas nodded.

Ten.

I leaned in close. "You two visit often?"

He frowned at me, and I knew I'd better back off. My questions were raising his hackles.

Five.

Oh well. I didn't have any more time to pursue the subject anyhow.

"Hello, Thomas. I was hoping you'd wait for me. Our big event is coming up tomorrow night." Gertie did a little jiggle—think Jell-O. I almost groaned out loud. This gal's maturity level seemed to regress each time I saw her. Must have been Thomas's presence.

Thomas shuffled to his feet. "Gertie. Join us. I'm sure your addition to the conversation would be most welcome."

He pulled over a chair from the next table and held it as she took her seat. Gertie tittered her thank-you.

"We were talking about Polly." I directed this at Gertrude. "Were the two of you close?"

"No. I wouldn't say that. I think Polly-girl didn't like it that Thomas and I are such good friends."

Thomas didn't confirm or deny. His placid expression gave nothing away.

Gertrude leaned forward, eyes lighting up. "I do have an exciting piece of news though."

If she was waiting for me to pounce and beg for her to tell, she would be waiting an awfully long time.

Gertrude hunkered down, craning her neck and making her eyes all wide and dramatic. "I found out that Sue Mie really made a mess the other night. She apparently got the snacks mixed up and doled out the diabetic snacks to residents with no dietary restrictions, and sugary snacks to those who did. That's why your momma had such a reaction."

I bit back the question on the tip of my tongue. Hardy asked it for me.

"How'd you find that out?"

"Heard her talking about it with her RN. She didn't say that's what had happened, but I heard the RN telling her to make sure she marked the snacks so that such a mistake didn't happen again."

"Couldn't she lose her job?" Hardy asked.

Gertrude accepted the plate set in front of her by the server. "Oh, she's got her own agenda. I wouldn't be surprised if she tried to off one of us just to put Bridgeton Towers, especially Mr. Payne, in a bad light before the open house Thursday evening." She picked up her fork, eyes twinkling. "Mr. Payne doesn't know who called the police the other evening. I bet it was Sue."

13

With conversations buzzing in my brain, Hardy and I made our way to the cafeteria exit. I about made it to the doors when a lone figure in the corner made me do a U-ie. Darren sat by himself. None of that on my watch, so I made sure Hardy was following me and introduced the two men. Darren shed a shy smile for Hardy, who picked up real quick on the situation and cocked himself in preparation to sit. I stopped him midsquat.

"Darren, why don't you bring your tray—" I swooped down and lifted it before he could protest— "and I'll introduce you to my momma-in-law."

Darren's eyes darted away from mine. "Might as well, being as we'll be playing games together later."

Hardy patted the boy on the shoulder and kind of pulled him along. "No sense in eating alone. Momma loves people, and she'll sure love you."

Matilda didn't miss much, and as Hardy and I returned along the route we'd just walked, Matilda stopped her conversation with Gertrude and bestowed a wonderful smile on Darren.

"Come right on over here." She patted the seat next to her.

"Momma, this here is Darren."

Gertrude remained sullen, as if angered I'd dare interrupt her conversation. Thomas nodded his head in Darren's direction and followed that up with a warm smile.

Hardy slid a chair out as if to sit. Halfway to the seat, I yanked up on his britches. "Don't cock your hind end into that chair; you're coming with me."

"You worse than my momma."

I lasered that boy with my eyes. "I take that as a compliment." I turned to the others and saw that Matilda was going to make Darren feel welcome. "If you will excuse us, we've got to scoot."

Hardy shuffled his feet like a petulant three-year-old all the way to the doors. I had flashes of myself with a big old cattle prod zapping his hind end a good one. Maybe I could find one on eBay.

Outside the cafeteria, Hardy turned to me. "Can't a man have a chance to sit and rest his weary bones?"

"As soon as you do me a favor."

"What you needin' this time?" He flashed his tooth and preened. "You calling upon my charms to woo secrets out of the ladies?"

I rolled my eyes. "Um-hm. That's it. I need to know when Sue Mie is on duty tomorrow, and I figure one of these here residents is going to know the answer to that question."

Hardy froze. "You mean you really do want me to use my charms on the women?"

"Honey, the only charms you know is a lollipop brand. Let's keep it that way?"

Hardy spread his arms wide and hugged me tight. "Who else would put up with this ornery critter?"

"Someone had to marry you."

He yanked away from me. "I wasn't talking about me!"

I went for him, but he ducked, laughing like a

drunk man as he skittered off down the hall. It wasn't too long before I heard the cranky piano in the common area sputtering a tune. He probably guessed piano music would attract a crowd, then he could finagle a conversation or two to get his answer.

As for me, I headed to that second-floor storage room. After hours meant cleaning time for the cleaning crew. If that storage room was going to be open or unlocked, I figured I might find it that way right about now. Maybe I'd keep up a slow stroll along the hallway for a while to see who came and went from that room.

For thirty-five minutes, I hauled myself back and forth, putting my share of wear on that carpet. When a short man with long hair pulled back in a ponytail appeared with a thick ring of keys and pushing one of those plastic trash carts down the hall, I kept moving, one foot in front of the other, biding my time as he drew closer. It was the same maintenance man who'd watched me haul Matilda's stuff inside Bridgeton Towers that first day and not bothered to help. Sure enough, he stopped in front of the storage room doors and picked through his collection of keys. He popped the doors open, then he went back to push his cart through, leaving both doors wide open. I crossed the hall lickety-quick and took a gander inside.

The room held extra beds, headboards and footboards, lamps, chairs, trash cans, walkers, wheelchairs, and a couple of vacuum cleaners. In the far right corner, I spied the elevator and some gym equipment. Vacuum cleaners and mattresses cluttered the path to the elevator. Typical of people. No one wanted to push heavy things any farther than they had to, so they pushed it off the elevator and let it sit for someone else to reposition.

All this registered in my mind in the seconds it took for the ponytailed man to turn and notice me. I checked out the name stitched on the front of his work blues. CHESTER. "Yeah?"

"You think I could use one of them vacuums? My mother-in-law moved in yesterday, and her apartment could use a good going over."

He hesitated, his eyes going over me real slow-like. Made my skin wrinkle up in distaste. His mouth moved like he worked a plug of tobacco, but he didn't spit. Good thing, too, or I might have hurled right there on his feet. Never took with men who chawed the stuff. My Caleb went through a stage where he thought it was cool. Till instead of spitting, he swallowed. Ha!

I finally received a reluctant nod from the man.

I cocked my hip and plugged my hand down on it. "I'll take that as a 'Yes, ma'am.'"

His lips compressed, and his eyes seemed to darken. I'm guessing he wasn't too humored by me. Or maybe his hostility had more to do with an age-old struggle that I had no tolerance for.

"I don't even call my momma *ma'am*. Never will either. Take a vacuum but have it back here in thirty minutes."

"Right nice of you."

His eyes stabbed at me. I'd had enough. "You got a problem? Because if you do, I need to know about it. No reason why you can't be civil."

Chester's severe expression lessened a degree. He averted his face. "Thirty minutes."

I made my way through the maze of equipment and snagged a vacuum cleaner, upright, feeling the burn of Chester's eyes on me. I ignored him, but his attitude sure left me smokin'. By the time I made it back to Momma's room, I felt drained, as if the day had included a marathon and two workout sessions.

I sank into the recliner and put my feet up, sure that a nap would solve my problems. But I had to stay awake to deal with Darren and our promised game-playing session. I imagined that Momma Matilda had brought Thomas and Gertrude on board by this time. Being alert to possible clues would be imperative. Thomas especially interested me because he seemed like such a nice guy. Too nice a guy, if you get my meaning.

Things weren't going forward in this investigation. Maybe I was reaching too far. Hardy was right; one successful murder investigation didn't mean I should assume people had some kind of vendetta against Polly Dent. She wasn't a very likable person by first appearances, but everyone has redeeming qualities.

All that hall walking built up a powerful thirst in me. I rolled to my feet to fetch a tall glass of water, never so grateful for its liquid coolness. When I dropped into the recliner again, I closed my eyes and drifted away.

Hardy shook me awake what seemed like seconds later. I glared up at him. "What you think you're doing? Do I have to post a Do Not Disturb sign?"

Instead of responding, he plastered his hand to my forehead. "You sick or something? Two naps in two days. This isn't like you, LaTisha."

"I'm tired, that's all. You all waiting on me to start the games with Darren?"

"Sure we are. You up to it?"

"Of course I am. What do I look like, an invalid?" My brain felt a little fuzzy though, my mouth cottony. The last thing I felt like doing was hauling myself up from the recliner. I sucked in a breath and did a mighty heave. Hardy's hands were there guiding me up, but when he didn't let go, leading me toward the bedroom, I didn't resist.

He pushed me down onto the bed. "I want you to lay down and take it easy." His cocoa brown eyes, flecked with gold, stared hard into mine. "I'm setting up an appointment for you. You're not acting right."

Tears formed in my eyes. "You get me a drink before I run salt all over this floor."

He patted my shoulder and sat down beside me on the bed. "What's wrong, LaTisha?"

"Nothin'."

"None of that. You used to come down hard on our girls for telling you 'Nothin'' when there was somethin'."

I squeezed my eyes shut, trying to line up my thoughts. Why did my brain feel like Old Lou misfiring on a cold day? Old Lou's what we call our decades-old car that still gets us back and forth where we need to go. Neither of us wanted to put Old Lou to rest, but with her motor sounding like the hacking of someone with bronchitis, her days were numbered.

"Missing the babies?"

I shook my head and buried my face. "Can't think right. Things keep spinnin' around in my brain. I'm tired, too. Down-to-the-bone exhausted. Didn't sleep well last night, you know."

"You lay down, then. Darren and Momma are

waiting on me to get back. I'll tell them you're not feeling well."

Hardy moved to stand, and I grasped his hand firm in mine. Fear gnawed at the fringes of my gut. Fear of what, I wasn't sure. Hardy stroked my cheek, his gaze melting over me, letting me know I wasn't alone.

He flashed his gold-covered front tooth at me. "Want me to stay and tuck you in?"

I laughed at that, swatting him away. I kicked off my shoes and stretched out on the bed as Hardy pulled the covers back. He pulled them up to my chin and kissed my cheek, making me feel every bit the love and security I needed most to fall into a deep, dreamless sleep. "Keep your ears open for things about Polly" were my last words before I fell asleep.

14

Weak morning light spread its fingers over Hardy and me. My eyes popped open, taking in Hardy's skinny self and the thin white blanket cocooning his body. I blew in his ear. He didn't move. Probably all those ear hairs blocking the breeze. I blew again anyway and kissed his cheek. His lips poofed out on an exhale. This man slept like a mummy and with that white blanket around him, he looked like one, too.

I slipped out from under the covers and shoved myself to a sitting position. Cotton brain symptoms of the previous evening didn't seem as bad, but when I stood to my feet, I immediately felt off somehow, like lying on a hotel mattress after years of sleeping on one that fit your body to perfection.

The clock read 8:24 a.m. Time to boogie. With great effort, I dragged myself toward the bathroom, avoiding the mirror. No sense making myself feel worse. The steamy water did help revive me somewhat, and my mouth didn't feel nearly as gummy after I brushed.

I looked into the refrigerator and decided on a repeat breakfast of the previous day. Eggs, hash browns, perhaps an omelet. Cheese omelet, maybe a little onion. Green pepper was out since I didn't have any. Oh, to have a full refrigerator once again. I missed my kitchen more than ever. Missed my house.

I shoved away those thoughts and began prepping. Hardy poked his nostrils around the corner before I ever saw his body. That boy enters the kitchen nose first every time I cook, and I love him for that.

"You get on in here and sit yourself down. Is Momma up? She's gonna miss the cafeteria if she doesn't hurry."

Hardy cast a glance toward Matilda's room. "Guessin' she's sound asleep."

"I'll hard-boil an egg for her." After I put the water on to boil for the egg, slid Hardy's plate to him, and parked myself across the table with my own breakfast, I dove in to discover what Hardy had found out in my absence last night.

"You find out when Sue Mie's on duty here?"

His head bobbed as he chewed. "Today."

Before I could form my next question, he slung one of his own at me. "You think it's safe to have Momma stay here?"

I sliced a chunk of omelet with my fork and gave some thought to my answer. Polly's death had Hardy good and scared, for sure. "Best thing to do is ask her. If she's uneasy, we'll move her out of here, plain and simple."

Hardy froze, eyes wide and staring.

"What's wrong with you, you swallow your good tooth or somethin'?"

His surprised expression molded into a smirk. "Nope. Just remembered about last night."

I stabbed a bite of hash brown and eyed the bananas on the counter, considering a bowl of cereal. The water was sending up steam, so I dunked in an egg, covered the pot, and removed it from the heat. "You meanin' when you came in here and pestered me to go to bed?"

"Nope."

He paused long enough to get me looking over at him and smirked again. Um-hm, this boy was up to no good. "You better spit out whatever's swirling in that head of yours."

"Momma and I learned something interesting last night." Another bite of eggs. A big bite. He chewed real slow.

"Stop messing with me, boy. You're having way too much fun."

His eyes twinkled, and he swallowed. "Darren is a wealth of information. On our way to the common area to play games, I asked him about Bridgeton Towers's history. He mentioned playing games with Mitzi until she got disoriented—"

"I knew that already."

A knock on Matilda's door got Hardy to his feet. Sweet little Sue Mie stood there.

"I check in with Mrs. Matilda Barnhart."

Hardy knocked on his momma's door, waited, then opened it a crack.

His head swung my direction. "She's not here."

I shrugged. "She can be an early bird when she wants to. Probably already shuffled down to get breakfast."

Sue Mie's head bobbed. "I check there."

I wanted to ask Sue Mie about her supposed mistake giving Matilda a sugar snack but decided to let it slide. Maybe the stress of moving had added to Matilda's problems. I'd heard stress could do that to a diabetic. No use coming down on Sue Mie now; I was sure her superiors already had.

I aimed some different questions her way. "I heard your uncle was a resident here. Is he still here? I'd love to ask him what he thinks of the place." I remembered those daggers in her eyes. She'd thrown them at Otis Payne in the office after Polly Dent's body had been discovered. "Would love to know what you think on the matter."

Sue Mie's eyes flashed, then she stared down at the little plastic cup with Matilda's pills inside. She shuffled the pills in the cup. "My uncle dead. He fall."

"Here?"

She nodded.

"There was an investigation, wasn't there?"

"He got fine."

It took me a minute to unknot that phrase. "You mean he got fined?"

She finally raised her eyes to stare into mine. I could see the swell of darkness and grief curling in on itself. Sue Mie had a right to be angry. Without knowing the whole story, I guessed I'd be kind of ticked if the hallway railing came loose and knocked my momma unconscious.

"My family not rich. Lawyers expensive and money short."

"You work here when your uncle die?" My speech was starting to sound like Sue's. Amazing how easily one could pick up on the nuances of an accent.

"No. Mr. Payne hire me."

This messed with my mind a bit. Why would Mr. Payne hire her, unless he didn't know. . . "So you're telling me he hired you, but he doesn't know that it's your uncle who died?"

"I not tell." She looked at her feet. "I not want to."

I already knew there was no love lost between her

and Mr. Payne. Could Gertrude be right? Was Sue Mie setting up Mr. Payne, trying to destroy him and the reputation of Bridgeton Towers? Now why in the world did it aggravate me to know Gertrude had the inside track?

"You know, Sue, if it gets out that you are related to the last patient who fell here and died as a result, it could look to the police like you might have a motive." That was a stretch on my part since the police ruled Polly's fall an accident.

Her expression showed disbelief. "I not hurt Polly."

"But you wouldn't mind hurting Bridgeton Towers, would you? You blame Otis Payne for your uncle's accident?"

Sue turned back to her cart, fumbling with some paperwork. With both hands on her cart, she pushed forward, toward the next door. She fumbled around a bit, then she wrote something on her clipboard. I let her go. But watching her reaction to our conversation reinforced one idea. Nurses, doctors, CNAs, whoever, were all human, and when in the grip of powerful emotion, anything could happen. Even a mistake that cost a life.

<hr />

Hardy and me found Matilda down in the cafeteria, grinning from ear to ear as she chatted with a captive audience. Even Darren laughed at Matilda's story, probably something about Hardy's youthful antics. She'd warned me several times before our first baby that Hardy had been a handful. Most of our babies had enough of me in them to tame that streak she'd warned me of. Thankfully.

We settled ourselves out in the common area. I figured he'd go straight to the piano, but instead he plopped down on the sofa beside me and stretched his arm around my shoulders—or as far around as he could manage.

"You feelin' okay?"

I nodded.

"What's got you quiet? You're never quiet."

"Am too. You're always so busy flapping your gums you don't hear my quiet."

"Hard being here, isn't it?"

"Yeah," I admitted. I shook my head and tried to refocus on the elements of Polly's fall that seemed suspicious. "I can't shake the feeling there's more to Polly's fall."

He guffawed. "Shoulda figured you'd have your mind wrapped around a puzzle."

"Something's not right. Too many people didn't like her."

"Expect there are a few who don't care for you too much; that doesn't mean they want you dead."

I huffed. "I should have come right out and asked Sue Mie if she'd called the police."

"Why didn't you?"

"Didn't think of it."

If there's one thing I know, it's Hardy's ways. He was trying to let me down easy. Trying to get me to see that I should let the whole incident slide.

Hardy gave me a side hug. "You need to get back

and finish your degree. Now that Momma's settled, it's time."

I turned my head to look at him. "I want that."

He stretched hard and patted my knee. "You still thinking on the restaurant?"

Your Goose Is Cooked, he meant. That's the name of the restaurant, not commentary on my cooking skills.

When my former employer Marion Peters was murdered months ago, it came out that one of the newer members of Maple Gap, our hometown, had been father to Marion's child years before. Mark Hamm had since taken their daughter, Valorie, and moved to Denver. I'd almost gone to work for Mark right after I found Marion's body, but he made his decision to take Valorie away, leaving the restaurant with a FOR SALE sign in the window.

It tempted me mightily. One thing I loved more than a good mystery was cooking a storm. Course, I liked eating, too.

But buying a restaurant was a lot of money. . .time. . . dedication. Funny thing is, I think Hardy really wanted to do it.

"You thinking about it, too?" I finally asked him.

He grinned at me. "I sure could go for some of LaTisha Barnhart's fried chicken 'bout now. Why don't we go out to eat tonight?"

"Sure, babe." I stroked his arm and leaned into his warm embrace.

The buzz of Hardy's cell phone startled us apart. Newfangled thing. We still weren't used to having it around. Our babies were so worried about us traveling without one, using the everyone's-got-one argument, that the phone and service plan became our thirty-ninth anniversary present.

Hardy twisted himself around to dig out the phone from his back pocket. "Yeah?"

A huge smile split his face in two. I could feel my own smile growing.

"Hold on and you can tell her yourself." He held the phone out to me.

It turned out to be Cora, our daughter-in-law, wife of our oldest boy, Tyrone. Cora had given us a grandchild about nine months ago. Our first. Now we had three others baking. Cora with her second, our other daughter-in-law, Fredlynn, with her first, and our daughter Shayna with her first. All within a month of one another. Don't know if Old Lou'd hold up to burning up all those miles visiting grandbabies.

"Momma, Arianna is walking!"

My heart swelled with pride. "That's my little gal. Do tell."

"She finally let go today and walked two steps before she went down."

"Bet Daddy's bustin' his buttons."

"You know him. Starting to think he loves her more than he loves me," Cora bemoaned.

"Nonsense. It's them hormones talking. You call him at work and tell him to line up a babysitter, and Pappy and I will pay for it. Every woman needs to get out."

"Oh, Momma, you don't have to do that."

She wasn't fooling me none though. I heard the

wetness in her voice. Cora's tender heart and patient ways meant she'd probably pushed herself to the breaking point taking care of Arianna. "I do, too. You're a good momma, baby, and if you don't do it, I'll call up that boy of mine and give him the message."

She laughed and sniffed a little bit.

"Now we don't need any mama drama." How I wished that Hardy and I could go over there and babysit. We'd visit for sure as soon as Matilda got settled.

"I'll call him now," Cora said.

"And make it somewhere nice. You need to get yourself fancied up, make you feel like a woman."

"You're so good to me."

"We take care of each other," I responded. "Just wish it could be me watching that little pumpkin. She sleeping?"

Cora rounded Arianna up, and I spoke fool talk to her for a few minutes while she babbled back. Hardy got in on the act, too, buzzing his lips and making silly faces, as if Arianna could see him. Some of the residents who'd trickled into the common area sure got a kick out of watching him.

We beamed at each other after hanging up. "Little Diva is a chip off the old block," Hardy said, puffing up.

"Guess Grandma's genes are dominant after all."

He deflated.

Momma's entrance shut us both down when she declared she was headed upstairs for a nap. "And I don't want you all flapping around in there. You knows I can't sleep with noise."

Who's she kidding? Matilda sleeps so deep you'd

think rigor mortis had set in.

She trundled herself to the elevator. Hardy patted my leg and went straight at the piano. Since I had some time on my hands, I decided it was time to ogle the library at Bridgeton Towers. I could use a good mystery.

15

I heartily support libraries. The idea of an unlimited supply of books on any subject; what a way to catch a mind on fire for learning. Bridgeton Towers might need some things, but it had a first-rate library. Large print books everywhere. Nonfiction books took up an entire wall. Biographies interested me. Sometimes. Depended on the person doing the biographing.

Sitting cross-legged in front of that shelf was Darren. He seemed deep into the book spread on his lap, not even noticing me when I came up beside him. Guess the boy got into things pretty deep when he set his mind to something. Nothing wrong with that. I liked a person leeched to a task. I did wonder why Darren chose to sit on the floor instead of cozying up in one of the nice chairs in the reading area. I let him be and moved over to eyeball the selection of mysteries, pleased to find one right off by my favorite author. Even though I'd read it before, it had been years, what with school and all, so I figured I was due for a reread.

A couple of residents that I'd not had the chance to meet moved into the library. One sat across from me, a rather hunched black man of at least eighty, who turned his teeth on high beam as he greeted me, sat, and spread his newspaper open.

The little old lady used a cane and shuffled toward the romance section. I returned to my story until I heard the impatient ding of a bell. Little lady stood at the vacant checkout counter, her gaze on Darren's back. So Darren must be the librarian. True enough, he unfolded himself from the floor, carefully marked his place, and helped the woman check out her books. As soon as she left, he returned to his spot, giving me a wave and smile before resuming his reading. Must be a good story.

An older gentleman sitting near me seemed engrossed in a scrapbook-looking thing spread out on his lap. I strained my eyeballs trying to figure out what he was looking at. Old newspaper articles and such is what it looked like to me.

In the next second, he sprang to his feet, clutching the scrapbook something hard. Near scared me to death. He had such a shocked expression on his face. I leaned toward him.

"You having a heart attack or something?"

His eyes circled the room. Whatever emotion ruled, his trancelike state gave me the willies.

I lunged upward and took hold of his arm, but he blinked. When he met my gaze, I sent him a smile meant to reassure. He blinked and blinked again, staring down at my hand on his arm as if contact of another human could not be his reality.

"Darren!" I grated out toward that boy, trying to rouse him from his reading stupor.

"Darren! Get yourself over here quick-like."

I was grateful when Darren sprang to his feet like a jack-in-the-box.

"Coming," he acknowledged my plea for help, two long steps putting him at my side.

The gentleman didn't move an inch, seeming unaffected by the sounds of our voices.

"Is this man's zoning normal?"

Darren moved in front of the man and tapped his cheek with his hand. "Mr. Wilkins? Mr. Wilkins."

"He always acts like this?" I asked Darren.

Darren took the man's elbow on the other side, and together we nudged Mr. Wilkins. He managed to put one foot in front of the other without any problem. We made it to the checkout counter, and I realized Darren's intentions. The phone squatted on the counter. Darren swooped it up, requesting a nurse in the library.

The nurse with red hair came in first. ANE HOOLIGAN her name tag read, and with that fire on her head, I imagined she must have the personality to match.

"Mr. Wilkins," she cooed. "You come with me, honey, and we'll get you to your room and have the doctor look at you."

And again, I asked, "He always do this?"

She squinted over her glasses at our patient. "First that I know of. Did something scare him?"

I rehearsed the story of him bouncing to his feet, wondering if he'd read something strange in the scrapbook he was clutching so tightly. Ane just listened, her head nodding in rhythm to my words.

"Thank you for calling me." She pried the book from his fingers and stuck it under her arm, capturing his arm with her free hand and talking to him in a loud voice that captured and held his attention. "You follow me now, okay? We'll take good care of you, Manny."

Darren followed the departing figure of Manny Wilkins with deep sadness in his eyes.

"You know Mr. Wilkins, Darren?"

He shrugged and stared over my left shoulder. "I know everyone, Mrs. Barnhart."

"I told you, none of that Barnhart stuff; it's LaTisha, or don't talk to me."

A smile twitched on his lips. "Okay, LaTisha."

"Good boy." I directed my finger at the book he'd abandoned on the floor. "What are you reading that's got you in such a grip?"

This boy practically dove for the book, trotting back to me as he shuffled pages. "It's a history of crime from the nineteen hundreds to present. It's a two-book series. The other is from eighteen hundred to the nineteen hundreds."

That was more than I'd heard Darren say since we met. He was warming to his subject like soup boiling on high.

"I thought maybe it would prove the rumor around here about Thomas Philcher."

I quirked a brow at him. Was he insinuating Thomas might have a criminal past. "Rumor?"

His eyes trawled the room, and he leaned in close to me. "Some think Thomas Philcher is none other than Frank Billings, the guy who worked with Stanley Phipps back in the 1940s. They robbed a bank together and made off with almost a million dollars."

16

I finally got around to making use of Chester's precious vacuum in Matilda's room. As I pushed and pulled the thing around the living area, I rolled the idea around that Thomas Philcher could be a reformed bank robber. Sure, he dressed nice and all, and he had an air of formality that made me want to release a belch in his presence just to see how he'd react, but a bank robber? I realized how vague he'd been when describing his youth, really giving us nothing more than what he'd done before moving to Bridgeton Towers, and his reference to not marrying because he moved around so much. Made sense if he was running from the law.

I snapped off the vacuum cleaner and coiled the cord, all the while wondering if old Chester had burst a valve because I didn't return it in his allotted thirty minutes. Made me feel downright ornery. I stood the vacuum in the corner. It had waited this long. . .

Glancing around Matilda's place, I decided to finish the cleaning part, then I stopped. Another idea blooming. Gertrude had mentioned that tonight was the night of the big open house for Bridgeton Towers. That meant two things; cleaning crews would be out in full force, as well as the cook and her assistants—unless they catered the event.

I hustled out of the apartment and to the elevator. On the first floor, Hardy's piano playing greeted me. He'd drawn quite a crowd. Everyone loved a piano player. You talk to adults who took lessons as a child, and most will say they put up a fuss practicing and quit too early, but they had great regrets for giving up.

A smocked housekeeper with wisps of graying hair clinging to her cheeks vacuumed the gym. I stopped dead—no pun intended. Her ring of keys dangled at her side. Could Polly Dent have lifted the key to the gym and made a copy? In that case, someone wouldn't have had to let her in. Polly was clear minded enough to do it, but why would she even want or need to get into the gym after hours?

The woman in the gym went farther into the room, disappearing from my line of vision. I strolled right across that hall and into the gym. When her startled eyes glanced my way, I waved a hand of authority to show 1) that I had a right to be there and 2) she had no need to worry her head about it. She kept right on vacuuming.

The room seemed smaller than I remembered. All those mirrors gave me more of an idea of how I looked than I liked. How could people stand to sweat and see themselves doing it? I stood over the treadmill Polly had used, even hunkering down to see if the foil paper was still there. It wasn't. My eyes went over the machine again. Nothing seemed out of place. Safety key in place, handles covered with powder. . . I swiped my finger over the white stuff and rubbed it between my index finger and thumb. I sniffed at it, the very faint essence of baby powder evident. Next I poked at the POWER button. That's when the vacuum snapped off behind me.

"Ma'am, no one is allowed in here after hours."

So much for my authority ploy. "They leave this

a mess, don't they? Had wrappers and baby powder and towels everywhere the other day." I laid eyes on the trash can full of paper cups then skimmed over the mirrored walls, fingerprint free today. The hamper was only half full of towels this time.

"It's always a mess, but *you're* not supposed to be here."

I turned to lay a huge grin on the housekeeper. "I know that. Do I look like I have plans on getting *on* one of these things? I'm helping Mr. Payne investigate Polly Dent's death, and I'm wanting to see this machine in action."

She considered my words, though I could tell she wasn't impressed. I must be losing my touch.

"We've got that big open house tonight; why don't you finish up your cleaning? I won't be a minute before I report my findings to Mr. Payne." True enough, because now I wondered if the maintenance crew, or whoever took care of the equipment, had tested Polly's treadmill for a faulty belt. Weren't gyms and places like that supposed to have scheduled maintenance checks on their equipment? It made sense to look into it, especially since I'd found out about the last death from a faulty hallway railing.

I presented my back to the lady, eyeballing the belt on the treadmill, satisfied when the sound of the vacuum vibrated through the air. Against my better judgment, I peeked at myself in the mirror on the back wall. Didn't look too hot. I touched my hair, promising myself to get back to Regina Rogane's hair salon, Wig Out, in Maple Gap and have her give me the works. My hand on the treadmill detected a definite hiccup in the motor's rhythm, pulling my attention away from my hair. I stood there for a few more minutes, eyes glued to the belt, hand waiting for another hiccup. . . . Nothing happened.

When the vacuum switched off again, I decided to call it quits. Without a voice to tell its story, the treadmill wasn't going to release any secrets. Now this made me pure grumpy. Here I had a case to solve and nothing yielding any good clues. In bemused detachment, I watched the housekeeper wind up the cord of the vacuum and roll it out of the gym. She glanced back at me.

I squeezed past her and popped into the hallway, hustling myself to Otis Payne's office. If the housekeeper saw me heading that direction, she'd sure enough know what I'd said was true, but I also intended on asking about maintenance records of the treadmills.

Mr. Payne's door to the hallway was closed, but neither was Miss Pillsbury in her place. Now, I could sit and wait, but that's not my style, and I heard Otis talking up a storm. I stopped in the doorway of his office. His back was to me, so he didn't see me as he dramatized his end of the telephone conversation.

Being the polite person I am, I decided to wait for him to finish—besides, his end of the conversation sounded mighty entertaining.

". . .it's not like that at all. The press will be here, sure, but my records are open to the closest scrutiny. The other records can be altered."

A long pause in which he switched ears and did a long sigh.

"Yes, you've made yourself very clear, but there's

no way to prove anything. Polly was old."

I'd sort of leaned in close to get a better grip of the conversation, when Otis spun around in his chair. Never knew the boy had it in him to be so quick, but I was quicker. I leaned on the door frame, crossed my arms and glared, as if I'd just walked in and was disgusted to find him on the phone. By his suspicious expression, I needed to put on an Academy Award performance.

My performance began where every good performance begins. With my mouth. "You tryin' to push me out of this here investigation?" I asked in a loud whisper. "Because if you are, I've got a thing or two to say."

He blinked at me, face blank. The person on the other end of the conversation must have said something because he jolted and stared at the phone in his hand a split second before sealing it to his ear again. "We'll talk later."

Now I knew a couple of things. No way was he going to ask me what I'd heard. People with something to hide are going to play it cool and innocent. And I didn't plan on letting him do the questioning anyhow.

When the phone hit the cradle, I hit the chair opposite him, forgoing the sofa in case I needed to get to my feet quick. I crossed my ankles, settling my clasped hands across my stomach. "Rumor's going around that you didn't call the police the other night."

His eyebrows twitched upward.

"I'm thinking it must be true. And if it is true, who called them and why? Another thing, what about this handrail that pulled away from a wall a few years back and caused a resident to fall? Does that have anything to do with poor maintenance?"

He opened his mouth to reply.

I steamrolled right over him. "I'm thinking it does and that I need to look over the maintenance records of the gym equipment—namely, those treadmills." I racked my brain to think of some other things to lay on him. "Back to the original subject"—and for this, I got my finger to waggin'—"I've got me a load of people who didn't like Polly too much. I'm going to keep right on digging into this until I'm satisfied. It'd help if you told your staff to trust me."

Otis's lips smeared upward into a not-quite grin. His expression made him look more like someone with indigestion. "Mrs. Barnhart."

I didn't like the sound of his nicey-nicey tone.

"I assure you I did instruct my faculty to speak with you should you ask questions. However, the police obviously feel Mrs. Dent's fall was purely accidental, so I passed on that news and let them know they no longer needed to feel bound to answer *anyone's* questions.

"Well, I'm not done asking my questions, and I'm not so sure Polly's fall *was* an accident."

Otis Payne leaned forward, hands clasped, the veil of authority settling on him as he straightened his back and squared his shoulders.

I leaned forward and lasered him with my eyes. "Don't get all high and mighty on me, Mr. Payne. Nothing you say will stop me from doing my own investigating. Things are firing up even as we speak, and I'm getting to the bottom of it."

Otis steepled his fingers. "You'll do so and report to me your findings."

I hauled myself vertical. "Don't play with me. You didn't include me in your faculty meetings. Why should I include you in my findings?"

His eyes speared me through, his face flushing angry red. "Then you will be asked to leave the facility."

I was getting him good and riled now. I cocked my head and glued a hand on my hip. "I'm sure the press would find your words quite interesting. Might even feel the need to come over here and find out why you're harassing the relatives of a resident."

His brain must have kicked in, because his posture relaxed as he ran a hand over the sparse hair on his head, puffing out a breath. "Mrs. Barnhart, I'm quite sure you have your mother's—"

"Mother-in-law."

"*Mother-in-law*'s best interest at heart, but the police have concluded the case, and there is really no need for you to continue your, uh, investigation."

"We'll be agreeing to disagree, then." And before the red flush creeping up his neck in the ensuing silence had a chance to burst into his face and out the top of his head, I decided it was time to present my wide rear end to him as I made an exit. "You'll be seeing me around," I threw over my shoulder.

17

Steamin'. That only began to describe my temper as I left the office of Otis Payne, director of administration, Bridgeton Towers Assisted Living & Nursing. In truth, my flare of anger had more to do with my inability to put together the pieces of Polly Dent's fall. Sure, the police could have been correct thinking it was just an accident. But Mitzi's poems. . .the tension between Gertrude and Polly over Thomas. . .Matilda seeing Polly in Thomas's room prior to her fall. . .Sue Mie's obvious disgust with Otis Payne, coupled with the possibility she may have called the police. . .

Lord, send me a good old-fashioned clue to tie all this together.

Notes from Hardy's piano playing floated to me. I felt the soothing spell of his music and relaxed into it. By the time I saw him, head bent over the keyboard, eyes closed, I felt lighter. Stronger.

I closed in on the semicircle of residents surrounding Hardy. His eyes met mine, and something strengthening passed between us. Thirty-nine years of marriage, and we had a level of communication that defied words. The tune of the music changed to a hymn I recognized and embraced. "I will follow Thee, my Savior" flowed from my heart and out my mouth. I motioned for the residents to join in, and we made quite the ragtag gospel choir.

Song after song came and went, some prompted by the residents, others by Hardy, a couple by me, until the residents began to clap, one by one. I joined in, making good and sure each of them knew how much fun I'd had.

"We should get Thomas in here. He loves to sing and has the most lovely baritone," a rather tall resident exclaimed to her black-haired friend, who obviously sported a dye job.

Black Hair's response interested me greatly. "Shaw, Sally, Gertie's got him now and won't let him leave her side for a second. She probably had a party after Polly's fall."

The two women were heading out, but their words sank down deep into my brain. Apparently Polly and Gertrude's tug-of-war over Thomas had been noted by quite a few people.

I gave Hardy a pat on his head. "You do all right for an old man."

His brown eyes glared at me. "Who you callin' old, woman? I can take you on any day." He pushed back the piano bench and stood.

I smacked his rump. "Sure you can, cute stuff." I lowered my voice. "There's a vacuum cleaner in your momma's place that needs to go back to the storage room on the second floor over Otis Payne's office. Haul it back there for me and see if you can get into that room and have a look around."

We started toward the bank of elevators, my fingers twined in his. He stopped short. "I'm no detective. How am I supposed to know what to look for?"

"Ask some questions, then."

"How do I know what to ask?"

I rolled my eyes. "What's wrong with you? You

forget how to work those lips in sync with your brain or something? Ask about Polly. Find out where people were, what they know about the movements of others. What they think about Sue Mie or Otis or—"

"I get the message already."

"Then why you actin' like I'm speaking some foreign language?"

He shrugged, eyes twinkling. "I'm not good at this kind of stuff. You're the nosy one."

Got to hand it to the boy, he's quick. As soon as he saw my hand coming toward him to flick his ear, he backpedaled like the Tour de France in reverse.

"You shut your trap and get on with your nosing around." I raked him with my eyes. "And pull your pants down some—it ain't decent."

He placed his hands on his belt and gave a little shove southward on his waistband, chest bloated out like day-old roadkill. "Probably crack the case myself."

The elevator doors slid open, and he hightailed it inside. Good thing, too, 'cause I was fixin' to run my knuckles over that head of his. Worse than any of our seven babies, but the chuckle that slipped out of my mouth just couldn't be contained. He sure is a cute little thing.

Collecting myself, I prepared my attack on the cafeteria to see how party preparations were progressing. I pointed my nose in the direction of the cafeteria, lunch over now, when I saw Sue Mie coming at me from the direction of Otis Payne's office, head bent low. She'd have run smack into me if I hadn't helloed her.

"Mrs. Barnhead."

No. I wasn't about to correct her yet again. When I

saw her puffy eyes, my momma's heart started thumpin' hard. "What's got you crying?"

"Problem with work."

"You get in trouble or something?"

She squeezed her eyes closed for a second. "I always in trouble. But I know snack I gave your mother was labeled sugar free. More than one."

"Are there others on Momma's floor who are diabetic and had a bad reaction."

She nodded. "Six."

"You think they were mislabeled?"

"Yes. Same as previous night."

I let this sink down deep in my head. "You mean the night Polly got a sugar snack there were others who had bad reactions?"

"It happened two times now." She gazed deep into my eyes for a minute. Her eyes twitched up the hallway then down toward the elevators. This wasn't a gal looking for a quiet place but one on the prowl for a particular pair of ears. She made a sweeping motion with her hand, and I followed her past Otis Payne's office, past the gym, and down that short hallway to the service elevator.

"I show you something." She withdrew a key, plugged it into the keyhole, and we took us a ride up to that second floor storage area.

"There something there you must see."

My excitement grew. This was it! I just knew the big clue I'd been waiting for was within arm's reach. But when the doors slid open like the curtains splitting before a stage production, the starring role had been filled by none other than Hardy Barnhart. And he was getting his tail whipped.

18

Chester, of vacuum rental fame, was shaking his
finger in my Hardy's rather pallid face. Leave it to
Hardy to get himself in a scrape.

"You better make good and sure you've got your
will written before you put a hand on my man." I
steamrolled toward the dueling pair, picking up speed
as I went and wearing my war mask, the one that made
my children scatter like cockroaches in the light.

Chester held up his hands. "It's cool! It's cool!"

I took hold of Hardy's arm and yanked him close
to my side, then I gave that Chester the eye. "What
do you think you're doing, shaking your finger in his
face like that? Didn't your momma teach you any
manners?"

He jabbed his thumb at Hardy. "I was telling him
you were supposed to have that vacuum back yesterday."

"Well I didn't. It's back now though, so you'll be a
very happy man if you'll be remembering that."

It occurred to me that Sue Mie had been quiet.
When I speared a look in the direction of the elevator,
I realized she wasn't there. She must have slipped
away while I was busy with Chester. But why had she
brought me up here?

Chester scratched his chin and stared at me. Hardy
gave me a jab in the ribs. A covert jab. Something
was ticking in his brain, but Chester didn't look too
inclined to let us have a private conversation.

"He hurt you, babe?" I let my eyes slide over

Hardy's features. He didn't fail me.

His back to Chester, he rolled his eyes all around, looking crazier than a coot, but I got the message. Eyes. Rolling around. I was to look around the room.

"He got my back *up* pretty good, but I coulda took him *down* real quick. Took me off guard, that's all."

Up. Down.

Notions whirled in my head. Up. Down. Stairs? The meaning hit me hard. The elevator!

"You two need to leave this room immediately. I'm locking up."

Hardy took off toward the door as timid as a sheep. I wanted to howl my aggravation. I wasn't going to set foot out of this room until I was good and ready. And where did Sue Mie get off to? Why'd she haul me up here then turn around and leave? Or did Chester's presence make the decision for her? Things were spinning mighty fast, and I didn't like being the one having to hustle to catch up.

Chester glared back at me, so I did the only thing I could think of. I dug in.

"You come back here with Mr. Payne and let us have ourselves a talk. I'm wondering why you feel the need to be harassing us about a vacuum cleaner."

Chester went as white as milk then as red as a cherry tomato. Hardy peeked over Chester's shoulder and gave me a wink.

"I'm not allowed to leave this room unattended." This from Chester in a barely controlled voice.

"That's right funny. Because I'm not allowed to leave here either, so you'd best be fetching him in a hot second."

Chester's nostrils flared.

I huffed and stared down my nose at him.

As soon as he twirled on his heel, almost knocking Hardy off his feet, I trawled the room for whatever clue Hardy might be hinting at.

"Tish, over there." I followed his pointing finger to the elevator and waited for him to return to the door and give me the all-clear signal.

It didn't take long to pinpoint what had him so stirred. Right in front of the elevator doors sat a treadmill, quadruplet to the other three downstairs.

Hardy leaned away from the door. "I'm thinking someone could have swapped treadmills. What if the maintenance records aren't so up-to-date and Otis Payne—or someone—knows that?" Hardy leaned his head back into the hallway.

As fast as my feet could carry me, I hunted for an electrical outlet, found one, and gave the treadmill a tremendous shove in that direction. I needed to hear what the motor sounded like and look to see if there was some kind of identification number in case I ever got to glance at those maintenance records. Another heave and it was close enough to reach the outlet.

The motor purred without problem, the belt turning without catching. I finally found some sort of number on the underside of the post that held the electronic readout. T61.

"Get some of that white powder stuff, and we'll have it looked at. Maybe it's not baby powder," Hardy said. "Remember the 'Snow in the hand sealed her doom?' Maybe it's the powder stuff."

Had to think quick. I zoned in on kitchen supplies

and found a stack of Styrofoam cups. I tore into the package and tapped the handles of the machine so the powder would flake off into the cup. It didn't work. I stuffed the cup back in a corner and decided to use the hem of my shirt, rubbing it back and forth across the handles until enough of the white powder had transferred to the material to satisfy me. Good thing it was a loose top. I folded the material in on itself to keep my sample safe until I could get the top off and into a sealed bag.

"On their way," Hardy said as he ducked inside and rushed to my side. Together we wrangled the treadmill back into its original position. He almost ran the thing over my foot. When I reached down to coil the cord around the post, I noticed a notch in the belt that made me stand upright real fast.

Polly's treadmill belt had a notch taken out of it! I'd noticed it the day Otis had let me nose around the gym.

Hardy tugged on my arm, eyes wild. When Chester appeared in the doorway, Otis on his heels, Hardy and I were back in our original positions, awaiting Otis and friends.

19

After changing my shirt and putting it into a plastic bag, I strolled from the bedroom to see Hardy sitting dejectedly on the sofa. "Thought Otis was gonna blow for sure. Good thing you had the phone on you. Never been so glad to have one of my babies call and say she'd been fired and was coming home."

When Hardy didn't respond, I knew what he was thinking as sure as I knew what brand underwear he preferred.

"She'll be fine, you know," I tried to soothe him.

"Not worried about Momma right now."

I frowned. "You think I didn't know that? You're stewin' on Lela's problems, and I don't think it's worth your energy."

He sank his head into his hands. "You think it's time to go home?"

What brought this on? "Do you?"

"Hate it that our little girl got fired. Maybe we should be there when she comes home." He turned his head in profile, jaw working hard.

"She's big enough to be on her own, Hardy Barnhart. Coming home doesn't mean her folks need to be droppin' everything that's important to them, and your momma needs us right now."

Hardy gave a single nod of his head, but his clenched hands told a different story.

I sank down beside him and pulled him into the circle of my arms. "What's the real problem, Hardy Barnhart?"

Beneath my hand, his shoulders slumped. "I'm worried about you."

"What you talking about?"

"You've been having those spells, though you've seemed pretty good today. Lookin' at Momma and how weak she's become. . .guess I'm feeling my age and hopin' I won't have to be spending my days without you."

"I ain't going anywhere anytime soon, so don't be plannin' no funeral."

His voice came to me muffled, his face against my chest as it was. "Do you think we should take Momma home with us?"

"It was her decision to come here, and I think as long as she wants to be independent, we need to let her be independent."

"Tisha?"

That tone of voice lit up flares in my mind.

"I made an appointment with the doctor here in town tomorrow. I want to know what's going on with you."

I opened my mouth, a billion protests and excuses rolling in my head. My eyes and mouth closed at the same time. If things were reversed, yes, I'd do the same thing. Force the issue. Make sure my man was okay and prepared to live a good long life.

I hugged him closer. "Not happy about it, but I guess doctor appointments don't generally make us happy." People poking and prodding around—they'd better have a real good reason to be doing it. I figured the strange things I'd been feeling lately warranted a good prodding session. Though I dreaded it.

"Thanks for rescuing me from Chester. That man's crazy."

I patted Hardy's shoulder. "Tell me what you think of all this. What does that treadmill mean? And Sue Mie is the reason I got to you before Chester'd reduced you to a puddle, but she disappeared real quick."

"Why'd she take you up there then leave?"

I settled down on that question like a hen on a nest. Here I'd gone and prayed for a good, solid clue, and things got even murkier, though the treadmill problem seemed a great clue. *Thank You, Lord Jesus.* "Got any ideas on who we can ask to have that white powder on my shirt looked at? The local police here'll think we're stirring up trouble."

"When did Lela say she'd be in?"

"Day after tomorrow," I answered.

"Then why don't we go home for the night and give it over to Chief Conrad? He'll help us out."

Sure enough. Chief Conrad and I had tackled the mysterious death of Marion Peters together, so I knew Hardy's suggestion was a good one. But being that I wasn't so sure how long the process would take, and needing the information as soon as possible, I made another decision.

"How about I go home tonight after this shindig, do some cooking for Lela, then go to our doctor in Maple Gap tomorrow. That'll land me back here tomorrow afternoon."

He sat up. "You going without me?"

"No choice. You need to stay here with Momma and keep your ears open."

He nodded. "I'll call the doc and make your appointment for you."

I waited as he put his ear to the cell phone. Since when did he have our doctor's number memorized?

Come to think of it, Hardy did have a mind for numbers. Not math, necessarily, but a mind for phone numbers and street numbers and such. When he hung up, I was ready.

"Got you in tomorrow morning at 10:30."

Oh yippee. I had better things to talk about than an old doctor appointment. "How'd you find that treadmill?"

"I walked into that storage room and wandered around a good bit. Chester'd just come in and caught me. He wasn't too happy. You'd think I'd broke into a bank vault or something."

Bank vault. "That reminds me of something else. Rumor is Thomas Philcher robbed a bank with another guy when he was young. Made off with a lot of money."

"Who'd you hear that from?"

"Darren. Think you could find out if it's true or not?"

"What you want me to do, come right out and ask him if he's a robber?"

I glared. "No. But you can talk about it. Look it up on the Internet in the library and see what you can find out. Ask Darren. Someone must know something."

"You find an identification number on that treadmill?"

"I did. T61. And I'm thinking hard that it's the treadmill Polly Dent was on when she fell, not the one in the gym now. The day Otis let me have a look in the gym, I saw there was a chunk taken out of the belt of the one Polly had fallen on. The other day when I looked things over, the belt seemed perfect, but that one in storage had a chunk taken out."

"Why would someone go to all the trouble to swap the things?"

I shrugged. "I'm thinking the maintenance records might tell the story."

20

Shocked my hair straight when I came out of Matilda's apartment and met up with Thomas Philcher, in the process of unlocking the door to his. His smile beamed warmth, and I wondered at the possibility of all that oozing charm being nothing more than a scam. He had to know the rumors going around about his being a bank robber.

He was dressed to kill, as always, and I could see where the rumor of his having money might have footing. On the other hand, it wasn't a crime to love good clothes. Or hats. Or shoes. Though it did cost a pretty penny. Ask me how I know.

"Whoo-ee, you must rob a lot of banks to buy such nice clothes." Problem with that great line was timing. My timing was way off, because I delivered it just as Thomas looked down to unlock his door. Drat. How could I analyze his expression if I couldn't see his face? "Maybe you could give my husband, Hardy, some pointers."

Thomas lifted his head as he twisted the doorknob and opened the door. I X-rayed his face for hints of subterfuge or dishonesty, but only that beatific, peaceful smile remained. "Though I would love to speak with you, Mrs. Barnhart, I'm afraid I'm not feeling well. Please, if you see Gertrude, will you send her my regrets? I tried to find her, but I just didn't have the strength to continue my search."

"Do I need to call a nurse or something?"

"That won't be necessary. I get these spells on occasion. I do hope you enjoy the evening festivities." He bowed his head in my direction, and the door closed.

Nothing frustrates me more than laying a trap that totally backfires, leaving me no further along than when I began. I'd have to leave the whole Thomas Philcher affair to Hardy's expertise. He'd know what to do. I hoped.

For the second time, I headed toward the cafeteria, determined to dig deeper. I tugged out the cell phone from my pocket and noted the time. Since it wasn't quite quitting time, I might be able to catch Sue Mie and find out why she left me on the second floor. Speaking of nurses, another nurse, one I hadn't seen before, trolleyed her cart down the hallway. Must be snack time again. Sure ate a lot around here.

"Do you know where I can find Sue Mie?" I called up the hallway.

The little brunette girl didn't stop moving the entire time she answered me. "Sue left the building earlier. I think she was sick or something. I haven't seen her."

That explained why Sue had looked like she did. "Are you new here, honey?"

"I've worked here for two years."

"Sue Mie's a sweet little thing. What's it take to be a CNA?"

"You have to go to school." She trundled her cart closer and knocked on the door. "It's not as long as for an LPN or RN. Eventually I want to go on and get my RN."

When the door creaked open, she exuded friendliness and efficient competency, checking off the name of the person before pushing her cart even closer. I could finally read her name tag. Kimberly. There was no answer at this door, so I decided to ask one more question.

"Is a CNA allowed to dispense medications?"

Kimberly shook her head. "An RN can do that, but a CNA can do it only if she's taken a Med Tech class."

An interesting fact that I tucked away. One never knew when a piece of information might come in handy. I gave Kimberly a wave as she prepared to distribute her next snack.

The idea that Polly's fall may have been the result of her medication had occurred to me before, but there was no way I'd ever be able to prove it without having access to records. Medication labels always warned against side effects, most including dizziness. So what if Polly's side effects kicked in as the treadmill was going? On the other hand, I couldn't shake the thought that such a side effect, even resulting in a fall, would cause death. Even if Polly had been fragile—and she didn't give that appearance at all—a broken hip, a broken arm, a concussion, yes, but death?

Downstairs, caterers in white coats moved all around, shuffling trays and pushing carts. So Hilda Broumhild had the night off. I stepped into the dining room and inhaled. Things were shaping up, and Otis Payne pointed and directed like the commander in chief he was.

His cochief sidled up beside him; I'd recognize those shapely knees anywhere, not to mention the blond hair and dark roots.

Otis seemed more irritated by her presence than

grateful. Of course, if someone was sucking up to me like a leech, I'd be howling. To his credit, Otis didn't shake her off, though I thought he might have been tempted. Deciding it best not to agitate him any more—a first for me and I was proud of it—I veered toward the kitchen and ducked inside after one of the caterers.

The doors swung shut behind me as my eyes followed the paths of the various white-uniformed people milling about. *Crazy* is the word that comes to mind. That's when my chest vibrated. That really got my attention, I can tell you that. It took me a second to realize my cell phone, in my breast pocket, was singing a tune and buzzing like a baby's lips. I punched the button and stuck the thing to my ear as I retraced my steps.

"You going to have to speak up," I admonished on my way through the dining room.

A reedy voice came to me, but I couldn't quite make out the words.

"Hold on there a second." I burst into the hallway, glad to have left the craziness behind. "What's that you're saying?"

"Mrs. Barnhart. It's Sue Mie, the CNA."

"Girl, what you mean leaving me up there all by myself?"

She knew exactly what I was flapping about. "Please, Mrs. Barnhart. I need to talk. Can you meet me tonight? There's a coffee shop down from Bridgeton Towers. If you go out the building and take a left, just look for it. It's called the Nuthouse."

Could have commented on that. Chose not to.

"I'll be there. What time?"

"Nine?"

"Order me a mocha with lots of chocolate."

"Thank you."

My return trip to Maple Gap just hit a major delay.

Hardy strutted around in his dark blue trousers and red tie like a banty rooster preparing for dawn. When Matilda appeared in her Sunday best red dress, Hardy bounced up to her, telling her how pretty she was and how she looked so good in red. It's a color I never touch. Makes me feel like a tomato. But red accents I can do, which is why my purple dress had crimson trim. Always did like the two colors together, and that's before the society of red hat lovers started up. Been thinking about starting a chapter in Maple Gap.

After Hardy sweet-talked his mother for a bit, he started in on me. "And you're looking mighty cute yourself, Mrs. Barnhart."

"Well," Matilda piped up. "When you two are done cooing at each other, we need to get moving. I'm hungry."

Hardy offered his arm to his momma. "You need to remember to watch what you're eating. LaTisha and I don't need a repeat of the day your sugar spiked."

Matilda took Hardy's arm, her eyes sparkling up at her only child. "You're a good boy, Hardy, watchin' after me like you do."

Hardy flashed his tooth that showed every bit of his pride at her words.

Matilda dragged him along as she hustled toward the door. "If we don't stop dripping all this sweetness, my blood sugar's gonna go up for sure."

I followed the two down to the cafeteria, hauling Matilda's cane since I knew she'd be wanting it later. She enjoys Hardy squiring her around, but she's also one to trot off on her own when she has a mind to.

The dining room appeared about half full when we entered. Otis Payne was mingling, greeting residents he probably never talked to any other time. I noticed right off that Mrs. Payne sat off to the side and looked ill at ease as she sipped from her water glass. Reminded me of our son Bryton. Never much for people, you could always find him hunkered down behind a computer that never required him to open his mouth. His wife, Fredlynn, made up for his quiet side. Bryton never attended a company party without Fredlynn to help keep conversation going.

Momma chose a table in the far corner. Not a bad choice, really, since I could see the entire room at a glance, but my goal was to talk to Mrs. Payne. I got Hardy's attention as he settled Matilda into her chair, and I pointed my eyes in the direction I was headed. Hardy nodded at me.

I greeted a few of the residents who'd sung with Hardy and me this afternoon, my eyes and ears cued for anything remotely resembling a clue, verbal or otherwise. The next table over, I stopped to chat with the two ladies who'd made the comment about Gertrude hoarding Thomas's affection and attention and settled down to some serious sleuthing. I started off by greeting the one I knew was Sally.

"Sure had a good time singing with you gals this afternoon."

The black-haired lady held out a frail hand to me. "Mary here, and Sally and I love to sing. Are we going to do it again?"

I lightly squeezed her delicate fingers. "You come on up and knock on Matilda's door, room 207. Hardy and I will be here a few more days before heading back, but we'll return often to visit with his momma. I'll try and schedule a sing-along when I know we'll be here to visit. That sound good?"

Sally piped up. "Love to sing. Used to have quite the voice, but age has made me scratchy."

"It was the smoking, Sally," Mary pointed out.

Sally squinted at her friend. "Best thing I did was give up those things."

I glanced around the room. "I don't see Gertrude anywhere."

"Oh." Mary did a little groan in her throat. "She's probably gone up to sit with Thomas. He doesn't need a babysitter, but you'd think he did the way she flutters around him."

So maybe the relationship was more one-sided than Gertrude wanted it to be.

I opened my mouth in an O. "You mean they're not a couple?" These girls had the edge on things for sure.

"Oh my, no. Thomas loved Polly. . ." Mary stopped and exchanged a sad look with Sally.

Sally nodded, picking up where Mary'd left off. "Gertrude's after his money. Thomas was a bank robber in his younger days. It's rumored he has a million dollars stashed away somewhere in his room. Gertie was born poor."

This was getting good. "He robbed them all by himself?"

Mary gasped. "Oh no! He had help."

"How do you ladies know about this?"

"Manny Wilkins. He used to be a cop. Said he recognized Thomas from a picture in a newspaper."

Newspaper! Did that account for Manny's weird reaction the other day? Had he read about Thomas in that scrapbook he was looking over? No. It couldn't be.

Mitzi's warning not to let "him" get away with it rang in my head. Did it mean I could disregard any female as the person who caused Polly's fall? Or was Polly's fall just a front for Mitzi wanting me to look into something else?

"Why haven't you gals just come right out and asked him?"

Mary and Sally exchanged a perplexed look. Mary's face split into a grin. "Guess it's more fun to speculate than to know the truth."

Sally's eyes drifted to something over my shoulder. "Well, lookie what the cat dragged in."

I craned my neck around to get a gander. Wonder of wonders, Gertrude Hermann drifted our direction dragging Thomas in her wake, his hand pulled through the crook of her arm. Thomas looked. . .*resigned* was the only word that came to my mind. Like a man made to go shopping in lieu of enjoying the Super Bowl.

"LaTisha," Gertrude huffed. "How nice to see you again." She bobbed a nod of greeting at Sally and Mary then returned her attention to me. "Do you know where Mitzi is? She gets testy if I don't sit with her at these occasions."

"I haven't seen Mitzi at all today. Is she sick?"

Gertrude frowned over at Thomas. "We'll have to check on her."

Thomas's expression seemed genuinely pained. "Of course."

I wanted real bad to ask Thomas if he'd been a bank robber, and usually I would have, but something made me hold my tongue. See? Miracles do happen. Imagine my surprise, though, when Thomas tugged his hand from Gertrude's grip and turned to me.

"Mrs. Barnhart." He leaned down to whisper in my ear. "Might I have a word with you?"

Gertrude's eyebrows shot into her hairline, and when Thomas helped me to my feet and she realized we were leaving the room, she made a move as if to follow us. Thomas put a hand along her arm. "I'm sure these ladies need some lively conversation, Gertie. Why don't you wait for me here?"

I trailed him through the room, which had filled quite a bit since our arrival. I waited as Thomas greeted the females who stopped him and the men who seemed intent on getting him to join their table. Not a doubt in my mind that Thomas Philcher was a mighty popular figure in Bridgeton Towers. Either his charm won everyone over, or the waggle tongues tangled up in the rumor hoped kindness might land them in his will.

We were almost to the doors when a trilling voice stopped us both in our tracks.

"Thomas Philcher, you scoundrel, why don't you eat with Otis and me?"

Mrs. Payne slipped up from behind us and laid a hand along Thomas's sleeve. This was the most animated I'd seen her since her imitation of a leech on Otis's arm earlier. Thomas smoothed his ice blue tie and caught Mrs. Payne's hand in his, presenting her with a shallow bow to finish off his greeting. This boy knew his way with women, that's for sure.

"I'm afraid I have another engagement right now. Perhaps later in the evening we can talk, Louise."

Thomas kept trucking, and I watched to see what Louise Payne's reaction would be to the brush-off, albeit a polite one. For a nanosecond, anger turned her mouth into a hard line and her eyes to pinpoints of light, but she recovered quickly. Without even a greeting to me, she returned to her still-empty table, slipping her skinny self into her seat and slamming back the contents of her tumbler of water. Or at least I thought it was water.

I fully expected Thomas to be waiting outside the doors, but he'd already scooted around the corner.

"Let's bypass the elevators and take the stairs," he whispered as I drew closer.

Um-hm. My meter went to full alert. If this boy thought he could take me down, he had another thing coming. I'd have to be careful not to let him corner me on the stairs, or he might get it in his head to give me a push.

I made good and sure to follow *him* up all fourteen steps to a landing—where I promptly rejoiced for life and breath—before finishing the remaining fourteen steps. With every step I wondered why Thomas couldn't just ask me what he wanted to ask me downstairs. Must be important. Or he was going to try something stupid. But I couldn't let my head get full of crazy notions, or I'd scoot out of here real quick and might miss something important.

Thomas opened the door leading to the second-floor stairway. I stood right where I landed, trying my best to suck air into my starved lungs. "I'm not going another step without knowing what you're wanting with me." I managed to get all those words out without gasping between each syllable, but if I had to move another muscle, I might send him for an oxygen tank.

"I'm sorry, I forget not everyone is used to steps."

"Honey, let's be brief with this subject. It's not the steps; it's the going up and down them that's the problem. I've got a set of steps at home; I go down in the morning, up at night, and that's my exercise program. You feeling me?"

Thomas cracked a smile. "Yes, ma'am."

"Now I figure we can talk right here as long as you keep your voice down a notch. You know the rumor's going around that you robbed yourself a bank when you were younger."

"That's part of what I need to discuss with you."

"Did you or didn't you rob a bank?"

He drew in a great breath of air. "I'm afraid the rumor is true. My partner and I robbed three banks in two days. I spent twenty-five years in prison for the deed."

"Thank you for settling that for me. The women here are clucking about it like it's the most romantic thing they've heard of. Guess they wouldn't think that way if it'd been their money you'd stolen."

Thomas grimaced. "Yes, you're right about that. But what I want to talk to you about. . .well, do you mind if I check on Mitzi? She is ill, and they're planning on moving her to first-floor nursing care next week."

"What's that mean for her?"

"It's more strict. For those who can't take care of themselves. I'd like to check on her before I forget, then we can discuss what we need to. Why don't you wait for me here?"

"Wouldn't mind seeing her myself."

Thomas's eyes clouded. "She's been agitated lately, Mrs. Barnhart. I really don't want to get her any more riled than she has been."

I got the message and settled my bulk on the step as best I could, content to wait, but when the door opened below me on the first floor and the voices drifted to me in hushed whispers, peace turned into a quivering ball of excitement in my stomach.

21

I'm not staying here another minute." The first voice came clearly to me. It was Mrs. Payne.

"Keep your voice down, Louise." Otis.

"I will not!"

The lady was out of control. I almost didn't make out Otis's next words.

"Were you able to talk to Thomas?"

"He was leaving with that fat black woman. What are we going to do? What if he tells her about the money?"

Fat? If I didn't have a good strong self-image, I'd have barreled down those steps and taught her a thing or two about sassy mouths.

"It's not a secret anymore, Louise. Manny confirmed Thomas was the bank robber, but he hasn't kept quiet about it."

A pause, then: "Then I want a share of the other money, and if you don't get that money for me, Otis, you can kiss me good-bye. I won't be poor another day. Now, I've got an appointment."

"I can guess with whom." Otis's voice had lost its wheedling tone. Now his voice cut like a hot blade through butter.

Louise blew out a gusty sigh. "Guess all you want. I'm leaving."

The creak of the stairwell door opening. "Louise." A rustle of material, and I could imagine Otis snagging her arm before she left the stairwell. "Don't do this to us."

What was this? Otis begging the leech to stay? I guessed the person she was so hot to meet must not be a good buddy, which would be a huge reason for Otis to suddenly be interested in his wife. Even pleading with her to stay when he looked so put out with her earlier?

Or maybe she knew something about old Otis that would ruin him if they split and got into a messy divorce. Was the money she demanded really hush money? Sounded like she had him over a barrel.

Otis must have slipped out behind Louise, because I didn't hear another word from below. When Thomas reappeared twenty minutes later, I was primed, questions at the ready.

"Mitzi is sick—real sick" were Thomas's first words. He didn't look too well himself.

"Doesn't the doctor show up when the residents are sick?"

Thomas cleared his throat. "He's already seen her."

Now, I can tell you there was more to that response than Thomas was saying. "It's time to drop the charm, Thomas. What's going on that you're so reluctant to spill?"

Thomas held the door for me. "Care to talk in my apartment?"

I wasn't so reluctant to move now, so we slipped down the empty hallway toward his room, quiet the whole way. I figured it'd be better to nail his hide to the wall in the privacy of his room rather than the hallway.

When I stepped into Thomas's apartment, the first thing I noticed was the woodsy, slightly minty undertone of the air. Very pleasant. And Thomas's choice in furniture sure crushed my sons' choices when they were single. Gold-toned chenille with a subtle print of turquoise, burgundy, and deeper golds shouted comfort and class. Dark wood tables of classic lines and a deep armchair with thickly padded arms completed the feel.

"You got yourself a lovely place, Thomas."

"Thank you. Could I get you something to drink?"

"Why don't we get down to business?"

He gave me a huge smile. "That's what I liked about you from the first. You get straight to the point. I tend to beat around the proverbial bush." He indicated I should have a seat.

I sank down into those cushions, hoping for an eject button somewhere, because when it came time for me to get up, I'd need all the help I could get. Don't they make nice, firm sofas anymore?

Thomas didn't sit but went over to an ornate hall table we'd passed in the short hallway near the front door. He dug around in the drawer.

"So you robbed banks in your day. Somehow I don't think your momma was too proud of that."

Thomas came up for air from digging in the drawer and favored me with a nod. In his hand he clutched a couple of sheets of paper. "My mother and father both died in my youth. My father from working in the mines for so many years, my mother from heartbreak. I was wild. I knew I was wild, and I didn't care."

"You were close to your father."

His Adam's apple bobbed, his lips compressed as he struggled with emotion. "Very. You're very perceptive."

"I enjoy people, and raising seven children didn't hurt none. What have you got there?"

Thomas closed the distance between us and held out the paper, a scribbled note signed by Polly. "After news of her fall, I found this on my hall table."

A puzzle piece snapped into place. Matilda had said she had seen Polly in Thomas's room prior to her death. At the time I'd feared Matilda's sugar level might have caused her to dream such a thing, but the hall table could easily have been seen from the hallway with the door open. Only one question came to mind. "She had a key to your room?"

"And I had one to hers." He waved a hand toward the note. "As you can see for yourself, she feared for her life. You asked earlier about the doctor. Dr. Kwan is a man with a past, I'm afraid. He has had many lawsuits leveled against him for mixing medications that caused problems with his patients. I suspect it is one of the reasons he works here and not at a hospital."

I read the note over again.

> *Thomas, we need to talk. Your past is known, and there are certain people who are desperate for your money. Trust no one.*
> *Love, Polly*

"You're telling me this because. . ."

"I read the article about how you helped catch a criminal in Maple Gap. I dug around a bit and found some newspaper articles on the death of Marion Peters. That was enough for me to know I wanted you to look into this matter for me." He closed his eyes and held out the second sheet of paper. "There is something else, too. Before the locks on Polly's rooms were changed, right after I heard of her fall, I went to her room and found this. Apparently she'd received a threat from someone telling her to back off."

The paper's spidery creases meant it had been balled up and smoothed out, and the person who wrote the note didn't want anyone to find out who he was—the words had been cut from a magazine or newspaper and glued to the paper.

> *Stop pushing so hard, or I might just push back. No one would miss you.*

I can tell you my heart raced with excitement. This proved what I needed it to prove—a motive. Someone had a reason to off Polly. "You brought me up here to ask me to look into things?" I gave him a hard stare. "Who's to believe you didn't have something to do with Polly's death? Did she know of your bank robber days?"

Thomas stared down at his hands. "She did. I told her. I thought she might be the one I'd waited for all my life."

"You thought? Something make you think maybe you'd been wrong in that assumption?"

Another long pause and I felt the vibes of rebellion—or hurt—that caused someone to be reluctant to admit his judgment of someone had blinded him.

He sighed. "She became very close with Mr. Payne."

Bingo! Though the idea of Otis Payne and Polly

Dent cuddling up to each other. . . Nah. "Tell me about it."

"You'll remember the first day you arrived here. At the elevators. Gertrude mentioned Polly and Otis rounding out our little group. I'm afraid it was intended to be a dig at Polly, but it is well known that Polly and Gertrude held no love for each other."

"Truer words were never spoken. I picked up on that catfight right off."

Thomas folded himself into the armchair and cradled his forehead in his hand. "It *was* true. Polly and Otis spent a lot of time together. I think it's how she got into the gym that afternoon after hours."

"Mm-hm."

"Our relationship wasn't. . .well. . ." He ducked his face into the cradle of his hand again.

"I'm getting you, honey. And I doubt Polly's relationship with Otis was that way."

His eyes burned into mine. "That's the reason I asked you to look into things. Polly never talked much about Mr. Payne, but the two did treat each other with more familiarity than Otis treated the other residents."

I smacked my lips together, powerful thirsty all of a sudden. "Think I could get a drink?"

Thomas snapped to his feet. "Most certainly. What would you like?"

"Water is fine."

While Thomas fiddled away in the kitchen, I absorbed what I'd heard and studied the note to Polly real hard. Who'd do such a thing? With great care, I lifted the note from the table, wondering if Thomas's fingerprints had obliterated all the others. I could drop this off to Chief Conrad when I got to Maple Gap, but unless one of the residents had a record, like Thomas, his or her fingerprints wouldn't be on file.

The print, too, might help. Whoever had prepared the note snipped whole words instead of letters. But that kind of search could be time-consuming, and if the person had been smart enough to get rid of the magazine or newspaper, it could be impossible.

I kept coming back to Thomas's money and the doctor mixing up medications. But Thomas's confession also made things more difficult. What if his confession was elaborate bait on a hook meant to force me to reveal what I knew? A tangled web.

When Thomas reappeared with my water, I upended the glass and gulped it down. "You have a baggie I can slip this into? I'm thinking I'd better take it with me."

"Of course, let me get one for you."

He returned with a sandwich bag, and I slipped the note inside and zip sealed it shut. "What made you show up downstairs? I thought you weren't feeling well."

"I'm not. Gertrude insisted I attend, and she does have a tendency to get her way, but now I think I'll call it a night."

I started rocking. Where was the eject button? On the third rock forward, I tried to haul myself off the sofa. Thomas, bless him, saw my dilemma and aided my ascent. After straightening my clothes, I eyeballed the former bank robber, giving him a wide smile. "Gertie's not going to be a happy woman if you cut out on her."

Thomas rolled his eyes. "Gertie's never happy."

22

Dinner was served. My stomach gurgled and popped in response. At our table, Matilda, Hardy, and Gertrude had tucked into their food, looking for all the world like a nice cozy trio of old friends. When Gertie saw me coming though, her eyes brightened and she looked ready to pounce on me. She probably wouldn't wait until my rear touched down either, which is why I bent to whisper to Hardy before her barrage of words left me no opening.

"I'm not just hot; I'm on fire."

Hardy's big eyes rolled my way. "I could have told you that."

He's such a cheeky thing. I patted his head and waited for him to haul his carcass out of his seat and pull out my chair. He didn't get the message at all, just kept grinning at me.

"You gonna hold the chair for me or not?"

He reached out a hand and gripped the seat. "I'm holding it."

Matilda came to my rescue.

"You pull out that chair for my daughter-in-law, or she'll be a widow quicker than you can say your good-byes."

Go, Momma! A woman after my own heart. . .and mouth.

Hardy's smile melted, but he hopped to his feet real quick, all the time charming me with those puppy dog eyes. Long lashes. Gold flecks mixed with cocoa brown.

Made my knees go weak and made me glad I had a chair to fall into.

"Where's Thomas?" The attack from Gertrude began with that simple question.

"He wasn't feeling well."

Her lip pooched, and her chins folded, triplicates of each other.

"He promised me. I hope you didn't call the doctor. Did he tell you about him? Almost no one trusts him. Not since Sue Mie's uncle died."

For all her brashness, Gertrude could pout like an oversize image of Nellie Oleson, straight out of *Little House on the Prairie*, though her black and gray hair scared away that image pretty fast. Other than her quick mouth, I knew little about Gertrude. Brashness oftentimes covered natural impatience or deeper insecurity. I skipped down that mental path for a second before Hardy got his tongue wagging.

"Gertrude and I were having a good talk over the old days. Seems we both know something about being poor."

"I did my best." Momma defended herself unnecessarily. Whenever Hardy alluded to his childhood and not having much, Matilda got quick on the defense. To this day, it irked her that Hardy's father left them with so little, though she never once outright complained about being the one to provide for her son. Hardy and I often suspected that Momma's heart had been shattered so hard by her husband's abandonment it had left her sour on remarrying. She'd never even dated again. Of course, with a son as devoted as Hardy, she knew she would be taken care of at all costs.

"Were your parents together, Gertrude?" I asked as she forked in a chunk of the hand-carved ham the caterer was slicing up for residents. It got me to wondering how they knew what to serve and to whom, dietary restrictions and all that.

"Mom and Dad died within three months of each other. My mom went first. Had a heart attack. Daddy just fell asleep." She slurped her water and dug in for another chunk. "Me, I never married. Had lots of men after me, but I could never settle on one of them. Decided it was better to stay single and footloose. Hardy tells me you have seven children. That's about unheard of in our day and age. Guess you felt tied down most days."

My thoughts tripped over the reminder of babies squawking, then teenagers with an attitude, then their moving out to get an education or start their own nest. Those children had me either in tears or in stitches. Grandbabies would be my reward.

"Tied down in a good way, Gertrude. Children are the blessing of the Lord, or haven't you ever heard that?"

Gertrude blinked and became still. "My mother used to tell me that." She stabbed at a carrot but didn't bring it to her lips. "She always wanted a lot of children, but something happened, and I was the only one. Guess I didn't make it too easy for her because I kept whining about how much I wanted a brother. She would just give me that sad little smile."

Count your blessings. Name them one by one. I had a whole list of babies for the naming part. Hardy's hand found mine under the table. He gave my fingers a gentle squeeze that let me know he felt the gratefulness for our blessings, too.

I decided it was time to start dishing the questions. "Did you know about Thomas's bank-robbing days?"

Gertrude swirled a carrot through mashed potatoes and popped it into her mouth. "Everyone knows by now. He made the mistake of telling Polly. Polly thought she was so sly, but she couldn't keep her mouth shut for two seconds."

A uniformed caterer delivered a plate to me with all the trimmings. I tapped my empty water glass. "You fill up this here glass for me? I'm parched." And I had another gig tonight with Sue. That should be a mighty interesting conversation. Sue would know a little more about Dr. Kwan, I was sure, being a nurse and all.

Hardy sat back in his chair, hands laced across his nonexistent stomach. "Wish I had me a toothpick."

"You could use the strap on my purse to floss with. It's upstairs though."

Hardy puffed out his lips. "Guessin' it's time to make that appointment with Dr. Cryer."

Dr. Cryer is Maple Gap's dentist, and the truth is, it was way past time for Hardy to be seeing him. "I'll make one tomorrow when I'm in town."

Hardy's eyes went wide. "No use rushing things."

Gertrude's laughter vibrated her entire body. "I'm not fond of the tooth guys myself."

In her favor, she did possess a nice set of pearly whites.

"I've had two cavities in my life. Got good teeth from my daddy." A mound of mashed potatoes disappeared between her lips. "Didn't eat a lot of candy either. Mom and Dad didn't have the extra money, so

I grew up without it and really don't miss it. I keep telling Thomas to lay off the sweets, but he doesn't listen. You ask me, I think he misses his little dog. He had a little dog when he was younger. Got hit by a car one day."

She kept prattling. Matilda started to doze. Otis Payne returned to the cafeteria minus Louise. He continued where he left off, going straight to the tables where relatives sat with their loved ones or to the new faces that clutched pamphlets hailing Bridgeton Towers as a wonderful place to live.

Dr. Kwan entered the cafeteria, making me wonder if he'd been called to check up on Mitzi, though after what Thomas revealed, I doubted *he'd* done the calling. I glanced over at Matilda, still snoozing along. Hardy caught my eye and nodded toward his mother.

"Been wanting to talk to that doctor some," Hardy said.

"While you're gabbing, I'll take Momma upstairs and get my things together." I tried to communicate to Hardy with my eyes. "Make sure you ask him about how he dispenses medications to the residents."

He cocked his head at me. "Didn't you tell me that CNA lady does that?"

"No. I told you she wasn't allowed to do it. Only an RN, but I'm figuring the doc has to be in charge of things somehow. Just ask."

Matilda twitched forward in her seat, and her eyes blinked open.

Hardy reached over and patted her arm. "LaTisha's going to take you upstairs, Momma."

"Don't need a nursemaid, Hardy."

"I've got a few things to do anyhow," I said. "We can walk together."

She gave me the hairy eyeball. You can see why, when she regained her mobility after the stroke, things became tense. She grated over everything we did for her that she felt she could do for herself. Now, I have no problem with someone wanting to do for herself, but when that same person is fragile to begin with. . . it sure gets awful hard to get her to see the wisdom of having someone nearby at all times.

Matilda hopped up out of her chair like some spring chicken. Her statement was clear: "Get off my back," or in her case, "Get off my bunions." She had a doozy of one on her right foot. I told her about my bunion-removal surgery, but Matilda dug in and said since she'd suffered with it this long she'd go ahead and die with it. I'd like to think I'll never be that stubborn, which is why it bugs me when Hardy tells me he married a woman who had as much gumption as his momma.

When I left, Hardy had corralled Dr. Kwan in a corner of the cafeteria. The good doctor's complexion seemed somewhat pale, but it might have been my imagination.

Matilda slipped into her bedroom first thing, leaving me to do my packing in silence. I fetched the overnight case from the bathroom and emptied out the things Hardy always left inside, fearful of forgetting them should he take them out, and packed the few items I'd need for the night. Each bit of evidence or motive charged around in my brain like a bull waiting for the flash of red.

With the stash of my toothbrush being the last item, I zipped the bag closed. I gave myself the once-over in the mirror, noting the gray hairs encroaching faster and faster. It was okay. I could live with looking older—it was the feeling older I didn't like—but one had to do the first in order to qualify for grandbabies, and grandchildren were worth the price.

I ducked my head into Matilda's room, satisfied to hear her soft snuffling, and closed the door behind me. She would sleep through the night.

A surge of excitement lifted my spirits. Home. I was finally going home, and even if only for a night, it still signaled the beginning of the end of Matilda's stroke and the months of rehab. It would be nice to be cooking in my kitchen again. I also wanted to check on little Sara Buchanan.

Before we'd left, Sara's mother, Suzanne, had confided her fears that her daughter's lethargy might signal the return of the leukemia. I'd make up a good spinach salad for her, first thing on my return.

Mentally I flipped through the list of things I had packed and all I had to do when I got back to Maple Gap. The shirt! I went back to my bedroom and grabbed the baggie holding the shirt with the powder taken off the handles of the treadmill. I stuffed it into the side pocket of my bag and waited.

I figured I'd need fifteen minutes to get to the Nuthouse.

Hardy didn't appear in time for me to say good-bye, so I decided to call him, but the phone kept right on ringing, and I ended up leaving a message. "You got this thing now; why don't you keep it turned on?"

So what if I'm the pot calling the kettle black. As a matter of fact, my cell needed a good charging before it started that annoying beeping. I plucked up the charger and stuffed it in my bag then thought better of it and pulled it back out. At least in Maple Gap I'd have a good old-fashioned phone. If Hardy needed me, he could call me at the house.

I set my cell phone to charging then beat it out the door before anything else distracted me and caused me to be late for my appointment at the coffeehouse. I needed a good mocha.

23

I arrived late anyhow. Turns out the Nuthouse happened to be about a five-foot-wide hole-in-the-wall store crammed between a huge bookstore and a drugstore, and I walked right by it the first time. The clerk in the drugstore told me to go back the way I came and follow my nose. Funny thing, that, because I did smell the coffee before I got to the store but thought it was from the little coffee bar in the bookstore.

When I opened the door of the coffee shop, my watch read 9:05. Sue Mie waited at a small booth for two. Mm-mm. I can tell you that small booth was going to get stretched to its limits as soon as I settled my wide bulk down on the blue vinyl seat. Sue Mie waved a hand as if I hadn't seen her the first time and motioned toward my mocha. What can I say? The thought of that smooth, chocolaty beverage called to me like the sirens of *The Iliad*, or was that *The Odyssey*? Whatever. Literature wasn't my strong subject; give me science any day. And math.

Sue Mie and I eyed each other for a full thirty seconds. I don't know what she was thinking, but I was thinking about booths being made by little people. I could just imagine these petite people running around with their tape measures, sizing each other up as they put garish vinyl over flimsy pressboard. Sue Mie was a little person.

"I hope that table has some give in it."

Sue's brow creased in question.

"Because if it doesn't move now, it will when I'm done with it." To emphasize my point, I pushed my body into the tight little space, knuckles white on the edge of the table. "Better rescue those drinks," I warned. Sue picked up her drink and mine as I gave a great heave in her direction. The table scraped and creaked about five inches before I had enough room to finish maneuvering my body. When I got settled, I noticed Sue Mie's red face and that every person in the place had turned our direction.

I leveled a glare at everyone staring. "You best stop gawking and get back to your talking." I raised my mocha in salute to my little audience.

People ducked their heads and returned to their conversations. I took a nice sip of the mocha and had to admit it was the smoothest, most mellow I'd ever tasted. Probably better than the mix I made up at home.

Setting my cup on the table, I glanced over the iced something or other in the clear cup Sue Mie clutched. Probably Chai. Stuff made me burp, though my girls drank the watery brew. They even wanted me to make a Chai punch at Christmas. Not happening. We had a nice, tangy fruit punch instead.

Sue seemed reluctant to start the conversation; I had no such hang-up. "Best mocha I've tasted in a long time." I slurped to emphasize my words. "But this meeting needs to explain why you left me in that second-floor room by myself."

Her face morphed from an expression of shy sweetness to one of hard professionalism. The same expression you see on someone concentrating hard. "I am not a CNA, LaTisha."

"What you mean you're not a CNA? I'm leaving my momma at an institute that doesn't even make sure the people they hire are qualified?"

She put her hand up, palm out. "Please, let me finish."

In a nanosecond, I realized something else. Her speech had changed. She'd lost the broken English accent. Now that I gave it some thought, even when she'd called, her speech had been different. Between the swell of confidence in her demeanor and her change in speech pattern, I thought she might tell me she was an Ivy Leaguer and a lawyer.

"I'm a private investigator."

Whoo-ee! I ran with it. "Let me guess, you were hired by your family to look into the allegations that Dr. Kwan somehow messed up your uncle's medications, which caused his fall."

She chuckled. "Close. I was not hired by my family, but the person who did hire me wanted me to investigate Dr. Kwan."

"Are the rumors true about him mixing medications?"

She shrugged. "From what I've discovered, no. It is much more serious than that. That's all I can say right now."

I took another long pull on my mocha. "Why this meeting, then?"

Sue's eyes lit. "Because I know a kindred spirit. I've heard of how you helped with the investigation in Maple Gap and how you caught the murderer. Someone like that is someone I want on my side."

I nodded. Satisfied, I scooted my mug out of the

way and leaned as far forward as I could. "Mitzi Mullins is sick. Rumor is the doctor isn't trusted. You're saying there's no reason for him not to be trusted? If you want me on your side, I want to know the scoop, and you're the one to provide me with it."

She pressed her lips together.

I leaned back real slow and let my sweetest smile grow on my lips before trumpeting my next words. "You're a CNA at Bridgeton Towers." My peripheral vision caught the patrons' heads turning our direction. "Funny, you don't look like one. You look more like a—"

Sue Mie's hand snaked out and grabbed my wrist, eyes flashing a controlled panic.

I lowered my voice. "I'm wanting that scoop, girl-friend, and you'd better give it to me, or I'll blow your cover from here to California."

In the silence that followed my outburst, tension burgeoned between Sue and me. This little girl didn't like my ways, and I actually felt a twinge of guilt for backing her into a corner.

Before my very eyes, the hard edge of her face melted. Sue clasped her hands together on the table and stared at her plain, unpolished nails. "I've got to be honest with you, Mrs. Barnhart. I'm just building my investigation portfolio."

"How many cases have you handled?"

Sue's posture deflated. "One."

Um-hm. "Let me guess, this one, right?"

Her dark gaze reminded me of spilled oil. "I'm a single mother. My husband is in the service." Her lip trembled, and she lowered her eyes. "*Was* in the service.

He got shot and killed nearly two years ago."

Interesting story, but I wondered if there was more to it. Her lithe body and youth didn't lend itself to my vision of the stodgy old detective with years of worldly wisdom to back up his naturally inquisitive nature, let alone a married woman with a child. "Why a PI? And what's the deal with being a CNA?"

"Before I married I was going for my RN, but Phil wanted to get married before he left. Since he's been gone, I've taken courses to get a degree in forensic science while my aunt watches my boys."

"Two children?"

A smile tugged at her lips, coming into full bloom as only a proud mother's smile can. "Twins."

"Whoo-ee! You had your hands full."

Her smile went brittle. "Phil never got to meet them."

Before I melted into a sympathetic puddle, I knew I needed to continue my game of hardball. Understanding her motives for being a CNA at Bridgeton Towers had little to do with answering the real question. Why had she called me here? "What was it about that storage room, and why did you leave me?"

"I'm sure you noticed that the treadmill in that room is the one Polly Dent was on when she fell. Someone made the switch in machines."

Should I let on that I suspected that already? Even if her confirmation helped boost my confidence, it still didn't explain why she took me up to that room. I was the amateur, after all. "You took me up there. . .why?"

Her expression became cautious. "How do I know I can trust you?"

I rolled my eyes. "Do I need to remind you that *you* called *me* here?"

She heaved a heavy sigh and shook the ice in her cup. "You're right. I wanted you to know about my undercover work because I hoped you would help me." She sucked in a breath. "I think Dr. Kwan killed Polly because she was onto him."

Stunned, that's what I was. Completely stunned. But never speechless. . . "Onto him for what?"

She leaned in close and dropped her voice. "I. . . can't. . .tell."

I pushed in hard against the table until our foreheads touched, and my eyes lasered into hers. "Then. . . we're. . .not. . .a. . .team."

I'm not sure who pulled back first; all I remember was turning toward the front door of the coffee shop in time to see a brassy blond slink inside. I'd recognize that hair anywhere. Just as my pipes filled to honk out a greeting, it was like an invisible hand slapped down on my mouth and rendered me speechless. Good thing, too, because another person came through the front door right behind Louise Payne. Tight T-shirt. Jeans with a hole in the knee. Tattoo on his right bicep. Dark brown hair and lots of it. Definitely not Otis.

Louise barely raised her head as she crossed the room and swept across the vinyl seat of a booth adjacent to Sue and me. Speaking of Sue, I turned my head to see her reaction. Surely she would know what Louise Payne looked like. Sue's brown gaze met mine. No smile. No recognition of any sort to give away her inner thoughts. One thing I liked less than tea was a person capable of playing stone face better than me.

Sue gave me a nod and made her exit. I watched her leave, wondering if I'd made the right decision. What if she knew something essential to the investigation? Being a CNA gave her an in that I didn't have.

I huffed and slid farther into the booth, wedging myself in with my back to the wall so I could peek at Louise and Mr. Tattoo as he slid in across from her. At least with her back to me, I didn't have any reason to think she'd see me gawking. Mr. Tattoo faced me though, so I kept busy with my mocha, trying to maintain the show of a content patron relaxing for the evening. I couldn't let my brain jump to conclusions. After all, this young man may just be her oldest son. Or a friend. Or her little brother. Very little.

The barista served their drinks, blocking my view of the man's face but not the sight of Mrs. Payne's sandaled foot doing a swipe along Tattoo's leg. Definitely not a friend. Or little brother. Or her oldest.

When they started sipping and talking in low tones, how I wished to be a spider spinning a strand down to within hearing distance of them. I could only discern by their body language what might be going on. Oh—and the foot. She had shed the sandal and now proceeded to go under his pant leg. His upper body swayed in toward the table. She met him halfway, and they exchanged quite the kiss.

I'd seen enough. Their distraction also made it a good time for me to leave this place in the dust. Instead of crossing toward the front door, I wrapped around the back toward the bathrooms, hoping for an emergency exit. I found it, noted the Do Not Open warning, and decided I had no choice.

24

Police lights didn't flash in my rearview mirror, nor did I get pulled over. A good thing. I feared the alarm sounding at the Nuthouse would have the state's best on my trail. After hotfooting it through the back alleys to Old Lou at Bridgeton Towers, I slipped into the Buick and pointed her toward Maple Gap. With almost an hour's journey ahead of me, I wanted to hurry. I also wanted to talk to Hardy one last time and remind him to keep his eyes and ears open while I was gone. I never did like leaving and not saying good-bye to him face-to-face. A phone message didn't seem like enough.

I debated giving him another try on the cell but considered the late hour. It could wait until morning. Events were spinning fast and furious in my brain. Somehow I couldn't believe that Louise Payne would be so bold as to flaunt her affair openly and within such close range of her husband's job. Maybe I'd read things wrong, but no, the foot told the story. So did Otis's pleas and his ominous "I can guess with whom."

Sue's theory about Dr. Kwan doing away with Polly flared in my mind, and I mulled the possibilities. But without inside knowledge, I would have no way of proving anything with Dr. Kwan. Drat!

As Old Lou coughed along the road, I gave up to the silence of the night. Might as well tuck in and think pleasant thoughts for a while. Who knows, taking a break could even uncover a clue buried deep in my subconscious.

Instead of feeling tired, I felt stimulated. Probably by the idea of returning to my cozy little home and resuming normal life again, however temporary. Which reminded me I needed to get registered for my last few classes to complete my degree. Had it really only been three days Hardy and I had been away from home? Guess I'm more of a homebody than I thought. Or maybe I just missed my routines. I loved Matilda, but taking care of her for these last few months had drained me. Hardy felt it, too, I was sure.

When Maple Gap came into view, I breathed in the night air like a starving man inhales food. Old Lou chugged past the police station and Sasha Blightman's boutique. I checked to see if she had any new, cute hats in her front window. That gal just loved to tantalize me with a new hat. She even admitted it. But the hat on display was one I'd purchased three weeks ago. The price almost had Hardy pushing up daisies, but he recovered after I made him fried chicken.

Then there was Your Goose Is Cooked. The FOR SALE sign in the window made my heart beat harder. Hardy thought owning the restaurant would be a good move. I knew it. Could feel his excitement over the prospect of opening our own little cafe. Hardy's idea of heaven is being near an endless supply of my cooking all day, every day. Can't be mad at that, and indeed the cooking part was the least of my concerns. Thinking on the matter got me riled up. I put the subject aside. Plenty of time to be thinking on Mark Hamm's exclusive lowball offer to Hardy and me.

I turned onto Goat Trail Road and blew out a contented sigh. Home. Even the arching tree branches that shaded our neighborhood during the day and made me think of protective arms arching over it in the night filled me with joy. I needed to lay out the key for Lela's return home before I forgot. With so many things to take care of the following day, I might as well finish up at least one task right now.

Hardy and I kept a spare key in the kitchen drawer closest to the side door. I set down the overnight bag and snatched the key out of the drawer and slid it under the doormat. Is there any other place to put a key? With all the warnings about the mat being the first place a burglar would look, well, who did those people hiding their keys in those obviously fake rocks think they were fooling anyhow? Besides, Maple Gap's crime rate had peaked with the murder of Marion Peters then flattened back to such major events as a child accidentally throwing a baseball through the grocery store window. Just the way I like things.

I sat down at the kitchen table and let my eyes wander over all the things so dear and familiar to me. My pots, my pans, my stove, and my nearly empty refrigerator. The wall clock with a collage of pictures of our children, though Rhys, my newest son-in-law, wasn't in those since he and Shayna had just tied the knot not even a year ago—and her already expecting their first.

A good stretch-and-yawn session gave my legs the incentive they needed to climb the steps so I could get ready for bed. Not until I got to the top of the steps did I realize I'd forgotten the overnight bag. I'd just have to use a spare toothbrush and make do, because no way was I making the return trip to pick up that bag. Not tonight anyhow.

Turns out the only spare toothbrush happened to be the one with hard bristles that Hardy hated to use, which is why he left it behind. He never could throw something away that still had some use in it. It made me smile big when I imagined his look of horror as I used his brush. If I'd had enough energy, I might have planted a blob of something slimy on the bristles to accompany my story of using his toothbrush.

The coolness of the sheets raised gooseflesh on my skin, but being horizontal sure felt good. I slept like a dead person, which is probably why I didn't hear any bumps in the night.

"There's no sign of forced entry, LaTisha," Chief Chad Conrad said from the side door entry. He pointed to the mat at his feet. "I'm guessing your visitor used the key you so conveniently left under the mat. What possessed you?"

I sat at the little table in our kitchen, sucking on a mocha and trying not to let Chief see how rattled I really felt. "Left it there last night for my baby when she arrives. Got to head back to Bridgeton Towers this afternoon. Hiding it somewhere was the best solution."

Chief stepped inside and let the door close behind him. "Not the best hiding place."

"You don't think I know that?" *Now*, I wanted to add. "Couldn't have been anyone in Maple Gap. Everyone knows me and Hardy. What do we have that anyone would want anyhow?"

Chief took the seat across from me and reached to

pat my hand cupped around the mug of mocha. "What the two of you do have can't be stolen by anyone, which is the main reason I think it was either a new resident in town. . ." Chief narrowed his eyes. "Mac Simpson is our newest, and even he's been here for quite a while now. Or it's someone who knows you and wanted to leave a silent message. Tell me again what happened."

First things first. "Are you hungry?"

Chief grinned but shook his head. "I'd love nothing more than to eat your cooking, but we'd better not disturb too much until we figure out this thing."

Made sense. "I slept real good last night. When I woke up, the sun was just rising. I lay there for a while before I came down here to make myself a hot drink. I opened the side door to see if the paper had been delivered, and it was unlocked, the key dangling on the outside."

Officer Mac Simpson stuck his head around the doorway leading from the kitchen into the front hallway. "Haven't found anything, Chief. Neighbors didn't see anything either. Something else I should do?"

His boss waved a hand of dismissal. "No, you can head back to the station. Run those prints from the key through the database."

"Will do. I'm gone." His head swiveled my direction. "I'm sorry this happened, Mrs. Barnhart. If you get scared tonight, call me."

I didn't have the heart to tell him I wouldn't be here. My relationship with Officer Simpson hasn't always been so good, but we made our peace with each other during the investigation of Marion Peters's murder and had become quite good buddies.

His offer touched a tender spot inside me. I'd have to bake him a Derby Pie or something when I got back from Bridgeton Towers for good.

Chief tapped my hand with his finger, drawing my attention to him. "You clutch that mug any tighter, and your arthritis will flare up."

"You're spouting tales. I haven't got arthritis!"

He sat back in his chair and chuckled. As bad as Hardy, he is, getting me stoked up like that.

He slipped out his little notepad and flipped it open. "You were going to review the events of the morning for me."

It'd serve him right if I got mulish. Truth be told, I needed him—and not just for this investigation. I needed him for that shirt in my overnight. . . "Oh!"

His eyebrows rose. "Oh?"

I scraped my chair back and headed out the kitchen and up the stairs as fast as I could go. In all the hubbub of the morning, I'd forgotten that this whole breaking-and-entering thing started when I'd come down this morning to retrieve my overnight bag. I took it upstairs then decided I needed to wake up first and went back downstairs to heat milk for a mocha. I checked the side door for the paper and found the door unlocked and the key in the door. I wondered now if the intruder had left something in my bag.

"Get yourself up here and look at this," I hollered down to the chief.

His feet pounded up the steps. When he came into view, I pointed to the overnight bag. "I brought this up here this morning. It was by the side door all night. I was too tired to think about getting ready for the day and decided to take it easy and went back downstairs. That's when I found the key in the door and called you."

Chief put in a call for Mac to return and dust for fingerprints. When we finally cracked open the suitcase, the three of us saw the small note written in block letters right away.

Back off.

Someone's trying to scare you, LaTisha," Chief Conrad stated the obvious as he lifted the note from its perch and placed it in an evidence bag. Standing at the chief's elbow, Officer Mac Simpson took the bag, the T-shirt with the powder from the treadmill, and the two notes from Thomas. "Take this over to Freedom Labs. Ask for Trevor."

"Sure, boss. Should I ask him to run them stat?"

Chief grinned. "Trevor will process them fast because he can't help himself. Curiosity is what made him go into biochemistry."

"Okay." Simpson sent me a grin en route to the stairs. "Don't hurt anyone, Mrs. Barnhart."

"Impertinent boy." I smiled at the chief.

"He's a real asset to our town."

We left the bedroom and headed back downstairs, Chief filling me in on Regina, his soon-to-be wife, and her continued grief over the loss of her mother. "She still grieves so hard. Guess it'll be that way for a long time. She was Regina's best friend and confidant for so long."

"She'll be okay. You two settle down and start having babies, and she'll have the comfort of family all over again." We reached the first floor, and I turned to assess Chief's reaction to my words. Just as I thought. His cheeks were pink. "Lots of babies," I added for emphasis.

He ducked his head. "Not everyone can afford seven children."

I reared back and gave a hoot. "Honey, not even Hardy and me could afford seven children. That's what builds character. You learn to make do. Learn to work hard. Learn every penny counts and that weeding a garden has its own reward." I got off my soapbox when we made it to the kitchen.

"She wants four."

"And you?" I couldn't resist asking.

His grin went huge. "As many as the Lord will give us."

"Good, but you do it right and get married first."

"Yes, ma'am." Chief Conrad swaggered to the door. "Well, I think we've got everything we need, LaTisha. Call us if something else comes up." He raised his eyebrows a fraction. "You won't be here tonight?"

"Headed back to Bridgeton Towers after taking care of a few things around here."

He had the door open and was almost all the way out when he stuck his head back inside. "Hurry back. We sure miss having you around to sass us." He shut the door real quick-like. I had to smile.

With a couple of hours left before my doctor's appointment, Old Lou carried me over to the Bright Sky Grocery, where Shiny Portley did his best to keep the produce fresh and greet every customer who entered his store.

"We've been missing you around here. How's Matilda?" was his greeting to me as I pushed my cart toward the spinach. He swiped his hands down his ever-present apron and over his bachelor's belly and trolleyed his produce cart full of cabbages and bagged lettuce from the fruit section to salad fixings.

"Doing well. She's settling in okay."

One thing about Shiny is he knows people. He heard the hesitation in my voice and pounced on it almost as quick as I would have. "Has she had a hard time making the transition? I hear lots of things from children with aging parents: mood swings, stubborness, anger. . . ."

"And you'd think that was the parents talking about their child."

Shiny chuckled, starting his stomach to vibrating. "When it comes time for the kids to grow up and start taking care of their weakening parent, it can become a real battle of wills." He stacked another head of lettuce on the pile and started straightening the heads of cabbage.

I reached for a package of prewashed spinach. "Matilda's been real good that way, but it's Bridgeton Towers that's got Hardy and me in a muddle. A resident there had a fall right after we arrived."

Shiny held a cabbage in place and stacked the other heads around it. "Can't say that I've heard much about the place. I can ask around though. There's bound to be someone in Maple Gap who's had experience with Bridgeton Towers."

Now why hadn't I thought about that? With Bridgeton Towers being less than an hour outside Maple Gap, surely someone around here knew of the place and its reputation.

"Might want to check the *Distant Echo* office. Michael would know of any rumors."

I bagged a red onion, the lightbulb shining bright in my head. Michael, editor of Maple Gap's weekly paper, would have his journalistic ear to the ground. I grabbed some fresh sliced mushrooms, slid them into my cart, and mentally added stopping by the paper to my list of things to do.

"You cooking for anyone in particular?" Shiny's eyes held a hopeful gleam.

I waved my hand at the fixings for the spinach salad. "For Sara."

Shiny's eyes dimmed. "You haven't heard the news, then."

———

I made enough spinach salad for Lela and Sara, and then I did some serious chopping for a quick batch of chicken noodle soup. Within minutes, I had the broth and vegetables boiling, with the intention of adding the noodles later. I turned down the burner to let it simmer and headed out to the doctor's office, heart feeling heavy in my chest. Old Lou's driver-side door was developing quite a creak. I'd have to get Hardy to dab some oil on the hinge, or we'd have us a haunted house on wheels. Old Lou already had quite a collection of engine coughs and moans.

As soon as I set foot in the waiting room of Dr. Alex Icon, I came upon Lester Riley, dressed in his usual overalls and farm boots.

"LaTisha Barnhart!"

"How are the cows, Lester?"

"Chewing their cud and challenging the environment."

A jab at environmentalists worried over the

methane cows burp in a day. Lester had a problem with people worrying over such things. "Human activity accounts for 55 percent of methane production, and they're worried about my cows?"

"You train them to belch on cue, and we can fuel a power plant."

Lester slapped his leg and guffawed. "You're good, LaTisha." He worked his jaw and quirked his brows. "You thought anymore about taking a seat on the city council? You'd make a good council member."

I noticed the doctor's receptionist was not at her desk and wrote my name on the waiting list under Lester's. "Politics makes me crazy. Besides, I've got my degree to finish as soon as Matilda is settled."

"Think on it. With Mayor Taser expected to retire, we might have a seat or two become available."

He'd been after me for months to consider the council. I dared to voice what was truly my opinion. "I'd vote for Regina."

Lester scratched his chin. "She's got a natural love for it, but I'm not sure how the majority would feel about her involvement with the Taser campaign scandal."

"Forgiving. Regina did it for her momma."

"But you don't steal from a campaign to fund your mother's nursing home care."

Lester had a valid point, but I also knew that those who really knew Regina Rogane, owner of our hair salon, believed her when she said she intended to pay back the money. And she had, too, even while being the victim of our current mayor's wife's blackmail scheme. Which led me to another point. "Look how good everyone treated Betsy after her public apology about the whole blackmailing scheme on Regina."

Lester shook his head. "She couldn't help herself. Betsy Taser's a social climber without a conscience."

Tammy Lyons, the doctor's receptionist, appeared, calling for Lester. When she laid eyes on me, she squealed and held out her arms. "Mrs. Barnhart!"

I embraced that girl like she was my own. And she nearly was. She and Lela had gone to school together and been great pals. "Lela call you? She's coming home tomorrow."

Tammy smoothed her hair from her eyes. "She is? She's taking leave?"

"No. She was fired."

Tammy's eyes grew wide. "No. That was her dream job."

I shrugged. "Was. She said the pressure was hot and she was almost glad to go. How's your school going?"

Tammy had begun her first semester of college after working for the doctor over the summer and finally saving enough for tuition.

"All As." Her grin was huge.

"That calls for another hug." I gathered her slender form into my arms while Lester slid by us.

Tammy whispered into my ear, "Thanks for getting me the job. Doc told me your recommendation made the decision for him."

"All I said was true, too. You're hardworking and determined, mannerly, and pleasant. What employer wouldn't want an employee like that?"

She pecked my cheek and scurried down the hall. Since the wood-looking plastic chairs looked less than inviting, I mounted the lone armchair like a queen ascending her throne. My hose quickly went to work rolling down. Made me want to switch to knee-highs. Not often did I get a bad pair anymore, but when I had to buy the cheaper brand because it was all I could find. . . I sighed and gave the curled waist a tug.

If only I were home breathing the scent of chicken broth instead of the sterile scent of antiseptic. I wanted to be anywhere but here. I sucked in a deep breath and let it out, trying to calm myself. The spells of the last few days haunted me. Somehow, way down deep, I knew this visit would not end in good news.

26

I called Lela as soon as I got home. Her cell phone rang and rang. I raced through what to say in my message then decided to simply ask her to call me back. No use upsetting Lela without being able to explain, though I knew my simple message of "Call me, baby" would put her on alert. Usually I left pleasantries and the latest on her daddy when she didn't answer.

I mixed up homemade egg noodles and cut them with a pizza cutter, making them as skinny as I could. When I lifted the thin noodles and added them to the boiling broth, the tears began to gather. I blinked. Drops of salt spilled down my cheeks as I tossed the last of the noodles into the pot and turned it low again to simmer.

I swallowed, wiped my hands on the dish towel hanging over my shoulder and turned to the refrigerator. I split the spinach salad into two containers and mixed the dressing in the blender, dividing that as well. Lining the picnic basket with a dish towel, I slipped in the container of spinach salad and dressing, leaving enough room for the soup.

With nothing left to do, I sat.

The phone rang.

Lela.

"Momma, are you okay?"

"No, baby. Things are bad all around." Tears came full force then, a gushing, gasping fountain that choked me and rendered me unable to answer the questions

Lela peppered at me. I told her all about my doctor's visit. She listened close.

"Don't you tell me 'no use borrowing trouble'?"

I couldn't help it; my heart puffed with pride, even if her words pricked at me. "True, baby, but I know how I've been feeling."

"Then don't fret until you know those test results. God hasn't suddenly lost control."

"There's more news, Lela." And this hurt me real bad to tell. "It's not good."

She sucked in air. "Tell me."

"It's Sara." I felt the rawness build in my throat. "The cancer is back."

Lela went quiet. "Oh no."

"You got fired, but the good Lord knew there was certainly work for you to do here."

"I've got my bags packed already. Maybe I should go ahead and start out."

"I made up some spinach salad and chicken noodle soup for them. There's some for you, too."

Her voice got soft. "How long does she have?"

I steeled myself against another wave of grief. "Six weeks. Two months max."

Lela made her decision to come home immediately, the tie between her and Sara a strong one. They'd become real good buddies during the weeks and months of Sara's first struggle with cancer. Before remission and before Lela went off to college.

I told her I needed to go back to Bridgeton Towers. "Should be home in four days or so, and I'll join you in helping them out."

I sat down hard at the table and tried to focus on

the task at hand. Sara needed to eat. Even if she didn't want to eat, her family would. And Lela would be home. She would take care of them for me while I was gone. It was the least we could do.

Closing my eyes, I breathed a prayer for this grieving family. For hope crushed beneath the heel of a sometimes too-harsh reality. Sara would go be with the angels, but she wouldn't leave here unaware of how loved and missed she would be.

My experience had been the reverse of Sara's, my momma dying when I was eleven, but my momma's sister took good care of me, and I had no complaints, only a deep grief that I hadn't held onto my mother for a little bit longer.

I placed the picnic basket in the backseat and slid behind the steering wheel of Old Lou. The Buick, with its leather seats and carpet stains from Shayna getting carsick, seemed like a scrapbook on wheels of my life raising children.

It wasn't even noon yet, and I felt drained. This wasn't just about Sara, this was about the elephant in the room. The weight on my shoulders over the possibility of something really serious being wrong with me that the doctor had hinted at. A subject I wanted to avoid. Lela's council had been sound and true. Not a bit of use being droopy over what I didn't know.

Lord knows, and that's good enough for me.

I squared my shoulders.

I rounded the corner and pulled up in front of the Buchanans' one-story. Sara stood at the door as if waiting for me. I heaved my bulk out and did a wave in her direction. Her face beamed at me through the screen door.

"Mom, Mrs. Barnhart is here! She's here!"

But Sara didn't run outside and throw herself into my arms, and dread gripped me anew. It was the weakness. Her mother had seen it, worried over it for the last three weeks. Sara didn't want to eat, and even when hungry, she only picked, and then other symptoms. . . . I'd forgotten Sara's doctor appointment coincided with our delivering Matilda to Bridgeton Towers, and I chided myself for forgetting this baby.

I placed the picnic basket at my feet and spread my arms wide, sunshine beaming down on my head. Sara slipped outside, her movements slow, her face pale. She wrapped her little skinny arms around me as far as they could go.

"I missed you, baby."

"Mom made me go to the grocery store with her. Shiny told us he'd seen you and that he thought you might be dropping by."

Ah. That explained her vigil. "Brought you some spinach salad and chicken noodle soup. And I have a grand surprise."

Sara's head tilted up at me, eyes bright. "What? What is it?"

I touched the tip of her nose. "Lela's coming home tonight. She'll be here with you tomorrow."

Sara clapped her hands. "Oh!" She scampered back inside. "Mom! Lela's coming back. She'll be here tomorrow."

Suzanne Buchanan appeared from the back family room, gaunt, stress lines evident around her eyes and mouth. I held up the basket I'd retrieved, and Suzanne nodded, her wan smile speaking volumes about the emotions she held in check.

"Sara, why don't you take the basket to the kitchen for Mrs. Barnhart."

Sara's huge grin exposed the gap in the front. "I'm hungry!"

When she was out of hearing range, I faced Suzanne. The young mother fell into my open arms. We spilled tears all over each other, sniffling and whispering words of encouragement. Then we pulled apart, exchanged smiles, dried our eyes, and went into the kitchen to join Sara.

We women have a language that needs no words.

<hr />

As soon as I got home, I ate a bowl of soup and tried calling Chief Conrad. There were some things brewing, and I wanted to know if he'd heard anything about Bridgeton Towers that should set me on edge.

"Haven't heard of the place, LaTisha, but I think Shiny's right. If anyone is going to know something, it will be Michael."

I filled Chief's ear with all the bits of evidence and accusations, motives and strange incidents that I'd run across in the investigation so far, then I waited as he processed everything.

"It sure sounds interesting. If you were acting in an official capacity, it would make things easier. If you want, I can call the police in that town and—"

"No sense in it. If your friend Trevor finds something suspicious, then I'll know to tip the police off and hope they investigate, but most of what I got is going to be laughed out of the police station."

Chief agreed. "But one thing you can do is swallow that pride of yours and work with Sue Mie. She's got an inside track being a CNA hired by Otis Payne himself."

It wasn't what I wanted to hear.

"The affair gives Mrs. Payne a motive to knock off her husband, but not Polly. If Polly was great friends with Otis, as this Thomas guy indicated—and Gertrude, too—then maybe they were more than friendly?"

"With such a huge gap in age?"

"Stranger things have happened."

True. "I can't see Louise being jealous of Polly and Otis." It didn't feel right to think about Polly and Otis having an affair.

"Polly was getting privileges from Otis. Why?"

"She acted like she was, but that doesn't mean Thomas is right in thinking Otis let her into the gym. Maybe she got in some other way."

"Those threats, too. . . Why would anyone threaten her like that? Was she the curious sort?"

"I really didn't know her."

"Others knew her. See if she was a troublemaker. Maybe she knew more about someone or something than she should have, and that person was getting really ticked and trying to scare her off."

It didn't seem real to be hearing about death threats and the possibility of someone murdering an elderly lady. "You think I'm crazy?"

"I think, LaTisha, that if someone is planning to get away with murder while you're around, that person is in for a huge surprise."

27

About six or seven stores down from Bright Sky Grocery and Wig Out, I entered the offices housing the *Distant Echo*, our weekly newspaper. Besides the printing equipment, Michael Nooseman's "office" probably held the award for smallest working cubicle. How that man managed to direct a newspaper from a five-by-eight area, mostly covered with paper, pencils, and pens, with a desk and chair wedged in for good measure. . .it was a miracle he hadn't died of asphyxiation.

I stood at the entrance of his office, arms crossed, ready and armed to rankle my good friend. "If you think for one minute that I'm going to fit in there with all the stuff you have—"

"You stop eating so much, and you'd fit in here fine. It's the reason I stay thin."

Whoo-ee! He was dishing it out today. I never could recall one smile out of the old coot, but Michael didn't need to smile—everyone knew his crustiness hid a soft heart. Not that you'd know it by his verbal assaults.

Michael unglued his eyeballs from his computer monitor and spun his chair in my direction, eyebrows lowered like storm clouds. He saluted me with his coffee mug that said, 'Write What You Know. . .' with sheets of blank pages stacked up high on a desk. Editorial humor, I suppose.

He scratched his chest and sucked at his coffee

cup. "To what do I owe the distinct honor of your presence darkening my doorway? I thought you were out of town."

"Something told me I'd better come back and give you a scoop before your one subscriber gets bored with the drivel you print and stops paying."

Michael wiped his mouth on his sleeve, probably to wipe away remnants of the slurp of coffee, but I think the action also hid a smile.

"Your momma taught you better than that. Use a napkin."

His nostrils flared, and his eyes darkened. "I've already got her spinning in her grave like a rotisserie chicken." He pushed to his feet and squeezed between the edge of his desk and the wall, knocking a stack of papers over in the process.

"Hope what you spilled wasn't important."

"Nah, just some bills that need paying."

That gave me pause and I wondered, in all honesty, how the paper stayed afloat. Townspeople had speculated for years that Michael Nooseman's side business developing Web sites supported the newspaper. Maybe it was time to have a fund-raiser to keep the *Distant Echo* going strong.

"Got my copy today but haven't had a chance to read it. Had me some excitement last night and thought we might work an exchange."

Michael ducked back into his office and tried to pull out his office chair. He finally had to lift it over his head to get it free from the cubicle. "Why don't you have a seat? Got some hot coffee if you're interested."

"Any hot chocolate?"

"Have to be difficult, don't you?"

"You gonna get me a drink or not? Seems to me I could take this story of mine somewhere else."

"My charming personality draws you here. You can't help yourself. One cup of hot chocolate coming up."

"With a splash of coffee, if you please. I need another one, didn't finish the one I had this morning."

Michael grunted in mock disgust. Purely dramatics. He moved toward a small kitchen area in the back of the room. "So you came here to pester me into making another one for you."

"Easier than making a fresh one at home."

Steam rose from the cup as he poured then stirred in the hot chocolate mix. "Spill it before they nail my coffin shut, declaring I died of boredom. I've got a paper to run, you know. There's not a lot of time to have high tea with every citizen who waltzes into my office."

"I'm gonna waltz on your grave if you don't bite that tongue of yours."

His eyes sparkled a bit. There's nothing he loved better than a good insult match with me. Why do you think he offered me a drink? Because he wanted the visit to be extended. I suspect he does get bored with just computers and words to keep him company.

"You know we're trying to get Momma settled at Bridgeton Towers. What do you know about that place?"

With slow, measured steps, he crossed the room and presented my hot drink. "Bridgeton Towers, you say? Hm. . ." He rubbed his jaw and shifted in his seat. "Bridgeton Towers. . .now why does that name sound familiar?"

His eyes cut to mine.

I was having none of it. "I know you know something. You got a mind sharper than glass."

"A compliment, LaTisha?"

"Prelude to the threat on your life if you don't stop messing with me."

"Bridgeton Towers. Quite the subject of late. Someone asked me the same question this morning."

This morning! My heart skipped a beat as I settled my hands around the warm cup and mulled the gleam in Michael's eyes. This boy was sitting on some piece of information like a bee guarding honey. I was going to have to smoke his hive.

"I know you're not playing games with me. Who'd call an old has-been like yourself to find out about current events?"

"That'll cost you, LaTisha." He folded himself into a straight-backed chair. "I can get your news from Chief Conrad."

The gauntlet had been slammed onto the floor.

What did he think I was? Inexperienced at negotiation? Seven babies who all grew into teens. I knew how to negotiate.

I leaned forward, eyes wide. "If I tell Chief to stay mum because the whole thing is part of a larger investigation, who do you think he's going to listen to?"

Talk about being left out in the cold. I'm thinking Michael felt the chill already. But I wasn't done yet.

"And." I let the word linger a bit on my tongue. "Since you don't know what I know, and what I know isn't happening where you'd know about it, I guess that means what I know is going to stay what *I* know unless you want to know what I know. In that case, you'd have to let me in on what you know for me to tell you what I know." I took a nice long sip of my drink, reveling in the idea that I'd talked him cross-eyed.

Laughter is not what I was prepared to hear out of him.

"You're a savvy one, LaTisha. But I'm sure I've won this round. You see, the person I talked to this morning about Bridgeton Towers was. . ."

28

Hardy Barnhart!" I shut the door to Matilda's apartment a little louder than I should have, but with all the unused hearing aids sitting on dressers and vanities around Bridgeton Towers, I figured it probably sounded like the regular click of a door.

I huffed at the silence. "Hardy Barnhart! You'd better show your face this minute."

I'd stewed and fretted myself exhausted over Hardy's call to Michael the entire trip back to Bridgeton Towers. Okay, not really that he had called, more that he had thought of it before me. Couple that with all the fun Michael had at my expense while I was breathing fire.

I strutted to our bedroom and threw the door open. Sure enough. There he was, dead to the world in the middle of the afternoon. "You stop playing possum and rattle yourself vertical."

He stirred a bit, and an eyelid cracked open. "Weird to dream of a bellow fanning a hot fire and open my eyes to see you." Hardy rolled onto his back and sat up. "Guess it's that hot air that keeps me warm."

"Why didn't you answer when I called you? Then I find out this morning that you called Michael asking the very question I'd gone to him to ask."

"Made ya mad, huh?"

He hauled himself off the bed and planted a kiss on my cheek. "Missed you, baby. Never the same without you nearby."

I resisted the urge to forgive him, zeroing in on the

offensive pastel plaid pants he had hiked higher than a Puritan's morals. "What rock did you drag those out from under?" Just when I thought I'd exterminated the last pair of plaid pants from our home.

"Manny and me were jawing, and he was throwing them out. I told him I'd take them." He gave a vertical tug that should have made his eyes bulge. It sure made mine pop.

I reached out and gave a hard downward tug. "Can't be seen in public like that nohow."

Hardy flashed his tooth at me. "You can't stay mad at me anyway; I've found out too much good stuff."

Him and his insufferable grin. I was melting but not quite ready to cave. "You could have called me."

"I did. I even left you a couple of messages."

What? I whipped out my cell phone—or would have if I'd had it. I eyeballed the little table by the bed where I'd left it charging and flipped it open. Five messages.

Hardy had that look on his face. That ha-ha-ha-I-was-right-you-were-wrong-but-I-know-I'm-dead-if-I-say-it-out loud-so-I'll-just-grin look. His eyes twinkled, and he rubbed his nonexistent stomach. "That humble look means I'm getting a pie, right?"

Is it any surprise he can read my mind? "You're going to get down to business and fill my ears with your news, is what you're going to do."

He shuffled right into my arms and squeezed me as tight as the circle of his arms could reach around my size 24 waist. "I love when you talk to me like that."

I breathed in the scent of him and rubbed my cheek along his grizzled hair. "It better be good, too."

He pulled away, and we entered the living room. "Momma's downstairs with a gang of women doing a craft thing."

"I passed them in the common area on the way up." I crossed my arms, hoping to prod the conversation along a bit. Hardy could get contrary when he knew something I didn't. "You talk to Thomas like I asked?"

Hardy planted himself on the sofa and leaned way back. "Nope. How'd your doctor's appointment go?"

A question I wasn't expecting and one that defused me real quick. I didn't want to think about the doctor or his probing or his concerned look or the tests or their pending results. No use stirring the pot when trouble would brew whether I talked about things or not.

"We'll know after the tests come back."

Hardy's eyes narrowed at me, and we sat in locked silence for a full minute. I wouldn't look at him. Didn't want to be gazing into those eyes I knew so well. That knew *me* so well. But Hardy wouldn't push me. Not now at least.

"Didn't get hold of Thomas, but Manny and I chewed the fat for a long while."

His change of subject allowed me to take air into my lungs again. I shot him a hard look. "Manny Wilkins?"

"Yup. Said he didn't recognize Thomas right at first, but he did some digging around and managed to scrounge up an old picture. Manny's son brought him over his collection of newspapers with articles about Thomas during his capture and trial."

It gelled in my brain. The scrapbook he'd been looking through in the library. "He found something in those papers."

Hardy quirked a smile. "He'd been combing through the things every day, until yesterday in the library when he found a small story about Stanley Phipps. It appears his wife of ten years didn't care to be a jailhouse widow and put in for a divorce."

"So?"

"So. . .his wife's name was Pauline Phipps." Hardy's eyes glinted into mine.

Pauline. . .Polly? My heart began to beat real hard. "Let me guess; her maiden name was Dent."

But that wasn't all. Hardy had another shell to lob my way.

"Manny said one of the residents saw Otis Payne in the kitchen with Hilda, and they weren't shredding broccoli."

"You don't shred broccoli."

Hardy shrugged. "I'm no cook; how would I know what you do with the stuff?"

"You sure have eaten it all these years. Don't you pay attention?"

"With a beautiful server like you, why would I notice something like broccoli?"

"Syrup's for sure dripping from your tongue. What trouble have you gotten into?"

"I leave trouble to you."

To be honest, I was stirring trouble in my brain right then and there. I had some investigating to do. If Otis Payne and Hilda Broumhild were *shredding broccoli* together, then why was he begging Louise to stay with him on the stairwell? Why, for that matter, would he care to stay with Louise at all if he was aware of her fling with Mr. Footsie? It all came back to hush money. Louise knew something about Otis that required him to pay her big bucks to keep her quiet.

It just didn't gel. Something wasn't right. The whole relationship between those two didn't make sense. Did she want him to get money so if she divorced him she could get at least half?

Hardy dug around in the pocket of his pastel plaids and unearthed a piece of paper folded small. "Got me a note right here that someone left under the door last night. I knew you'd be wanting to read it through."

Now why did all the good stuff happen when I left?

He unfolded the note until it was only halved, then with a flick of his wrist, he whipped it open and presented it to me like a maître d' allowing a patron to admire a fine wine.

> *Mrs. Barnhart, I'd like to talk to you*
> *again. Things are getting out of hand fast.*
> *S. M.*

Hmph! My chance to redeem myself. Humble myself even. My stomach roiled at the thought. Humility rubs me wrong. I can do it, but it's pain and agony all the way. *Sweet Jesus, forgive me.*

Hardy stuck his neck out over the note to look me in the eye. "Who's S. M.?"

"Our friendly CNA Sue Mie." I folded the note back into the postage-stamp size it was originally. "She's a private investigator."

Hardy's mouth formed an O.

I warmed to my subject like a house ablaze. "I

found out the other night. Wanted to tell you then, but I couldn't find you. She thinks Dr. Kwan pushed Polly Dent because she'd found out something."

I paused, wondering how to tell Hardy I'd blown my opportunity to work with Sue.

He sank down onto the sofa, his expression knowing. "Why do I have a feeling you played Barney Fife and shot yourself in the foot?"

"Only thing shooting was my mouth, and I backed her into a corner. She refused to tell me what she'd found out about Dr. Kwan and Polly."

"You played tough gal and lost."

I glared at him.

Hardy patted the cushion next to him. "Come nest with me, my pigeon."

The air went out of my defiant sails, and I plopped beside him. He promptly bounced high in the air, acting like the momentum of me sitting sent him airborne. Somehow it didn't strike me as funny. Instead tears pressed in on me. Hardy patted my leg, and I pulled him in close against my chest.

I swallowed hard. "I'm ashamed of myself. Really. I had no use being so, so—"

"Pigheaded?"

I sniffed back the tears.

"Cocky?"

The tears started flowing anyhow.

"Mean?"

I gave his ear a good tug.

"Ouch!"

"You've no business harassing me when I'm spilling salt everywhere."

"I was just trying to find the right agitate."

"That's 'adjective.'"

"Well what do you know?" He sat up straight. "What's an adjective anyway?"

I dried my eyes on my sleeve. It was no use wasting time explaining. "Why don't we go downstairs and try to find some trouble to get into? You need to talk to Thomas like I asked you to, and I need to find Sue Mie."

He snapped to his feet and held out a hand to me.

It hit me then that Hardy didn't know about Sara Buchanan.

"Hardy."

Interpreting the sound of my voice, his hand lowered to his side.

"Sara's cancer is back. She doesn't have long to live."

Hardy closed his eyes and lowered his head. I slipped my hand into his, knowing he hurt for her and the Buchanans real deep. Just like me. Which is why I wasn't surprised when he squeezed my hand real tight. "Lord," he breathed. "Oh, Lord."

His voice choked up. My tears came on fresh as dew.

"Be with that baby, Lord. . . ."

29

Hardy worked out his grief on the piano, his fingers weaving soulful tunes that had no words but spoke volumes of his hurt and probably his concern over me. The residents listened in awe, as they always did. I decided I'd better get to looking for Sue Mie before quitting time, and I touched Hardy's head on the way out of the common area to let him know I was leaving. His gaze touched mine for a full thirty seconds before his fingers picked up rhythm and the notes caught the wind of a livelier beat. This was his way of saying he'd be okay. We'd shelve our grief, and as he'd promised after finishing up his prayer for Sara, we'd get this mystery solved and get home as soon as possible. Our one comfort was that Lela would be there for Sara real soon.

The seniors were trickling toward the cafeteria again, and I worked my way through, patting backs and sharing a smile, all the while asking if anyone had seen Sue Mie. Darren's boyish greeting and shy grin answered my question.

"I saw her at the end of the hallway upstairs. She was playing Bunco with a group of ladies."

"How is Mitzi?"

"She's pretty weak. I think her medication is making her sick." Darren paused as a line of women exited the elevators, pushing their way between us in a flurry of walkers and travel knit, aka polyester. At the rear of the group, Gertrude Hermann clung to the arm of Thomas Philcher.

Her head swung from me to Darren and back again, sweeping a pitifully thin ponytail back and forth across her shoulders.

"Mrs. Barnhart! Have you found out any juicy tidbits about Polly? Dr. Kwan was sure asking about *you* when I had my checkup yesterday."

"Tell him if he has something to ask about me, I'm his woman."

Gertrude tried to tuck a stray hair into her tightly banded ponytail and failed miserably. It sprang out like the ballet dancer of a music box. She shifted her attention to Darren. He seemed to shrink back against the wall, and I remembered what he'd said about Polly talking loud to him. I could see Gertrude being intimidating as well.

"Darren, why don't you join us this evening? Thomas and I would love to have you at our table," she cooed.

Darren's Adam's apple bobbed. His gaze shifted to me, wild and a little fearful. Strange thing, that. Gertie might not be the kindest-speaking lady—but fear?

"Darren's going to take me up to check on Mitzi," I interceded, slipping my arm around his shoulder in a protective gesture. "She's been sick, from what he tells me."

Gertrude nodded. "Yes, I should check on the poor dear." Her eyes fluttered at Thomas, and she picked up his hand and slid it through her arm as if she were the man being the escort. "We could check on her after we eat. Wouldn't that be a good idea, Tommy?"

Tommy must have worked hard to push a smile to the surface, because it was obviously strained. "That is a wonderful idea."

Gertrude placed her hand over his where it lay in the crook of her arm and started forward like a cruise ship pulling a tugboat. I'm guessin' Hardy and I look a lot like that sometimes. Difference is, Hardy doesn't mind my pulling him.

As we walked back toward the elevators to the flowing music of Hardy's latest tune, Darren got quiet. Not unusual for him, of course, but the way he kept glancing my way and being all fidgety made me think something was in this boy's mind needing to be set free.

I waited.

The elevator dinged its arrival on the third floor, and we stepped into a throng of ladies and gents waiting to go down. I recognized the black-haired woman from our singathon a couple of days ago. She stopped me. "We've talked so much about how we enjoyed singing with you the other day. Could we do it again? Sally and I want to invite some of the men to round out our little choir. Your husband does play so divinely."

"Sure we can, honey."

"Oh!" Her face lit. "Would tonight be too soon?"

"Hardy's down there on the piano now. You ask him and see what he thinks."

The group huddled in the elevator stirred restlessly. Sally, Mary's friend, held the doors open. "Come on, dear. We're hungry."

Mary flashed me a sparkly smile, dimmed by the reality of her yellowed teeth but still full of heart, and hopped onto the elevator. Her dark hair made her a stark contrast to her other companions with heads in various shades of gray and white.

"She loves music," Darren offered as he pushed away from the wall. "Guess Sue and the others finished their game." His hand uncurled to grasp at the railing in the hallway as I followed him away from the empty common area and down the hall to Mitzi's room.

"The doctor know what's making Mitzi sick?"

Darren hesitated for a "spit second." Now a spit second isn't to be confused with a split second; it's a little longer. It's the time it takes for someone to spit and the spit to land. Our son Caleb introduced us to this term when he was at his spitting-to-look-cool stage. He didn't stay in that stage long, because Hardy has a way of warming up a boy until all the moisture in his body dries up and spit in the mouth becomes a luxury.

Darren's spit second passed, and he pulled out a key and slid it into the lock on the door. Mitzi's door. He motioned me in first, explaining as I squeezed past him. "Mitzi gave me her key. She wanted me to check on her." He closed the door behind us and pocketed his key again. "She doesn't trust the doctor."

That again. I wondered if Dr. Kwan understood how much the residents distrusted him. Darren tilted his head at me. "I checked her meds. It's the same stuff she's always taken."

He stopped in front of a closed door and tapped lightly before swinging the door open. In the dim light of a small lamp, Mitzi lay curled on her side, eyes wide open and staring.

"Don't be scared. She looks like that sometimes," Darren whispered.

With a gracefulness I hadn't seen when he'd folded clothes, Darren tugged the sheet up around Mitzi's shoulders, straightened the collar of her pajamas, and smoothed the hair back from her head.

His tenderness touched me. This wasn't a friend caring for a friend; this was a man caring for a woman he loved. Mitzi, despite her frailty, must have been younger than I'd originally guessed, which probably accounted for her spryness. And hadn't he talked about her days of clarity with a certain wistfulness?

Darren's body might be twisted, but his heart was straight as an arrow. He finished fussing over Mitzi and shuffled to the dresser where her meds were stored.

"You're loving her, aren't you?"

Darren froze, then he stood tall and nodded. "I do. There's ten years between us. Mitzi thought it was too much, and I didn't press her because I didn't realize how much I really cared until. . ." He closed his eyes and turned toward the dresser, hand hovering over an assortment of bottles and perfumes. He clutched at a prescription bottle, tears welling in his eyes. "When she moves to nursing, I won't be able to see her as much."

Darren twisted the cap on the water bottle he'd picked up on our way into the cafeteria. He hadn't said much on our trip down there. My heart broke for him. Nothing worse than being alone in a crowd, and the cafeteria was sure crowded.

Matilda sat at her usual table. She greeted Darren with enthusiasm before returning her attention to the meat loaf. Gertrude and Thomas rounded out the table. Gertrude didn't seem to notice or care about Darren's presence, merely sending him a rather hostile look before she resumed talking Thomas's ear off. Thomas sneaked in a huge smile and a polite hello before continuing his charade of listening to Gertrude.

"Let's get up there and put on the feed bag," I said to Darren, eyeballing the buffet and working my hand into my pocket for some money.

"I'm not hungry," Darren mumbled.

Maybe our talk of Mitzi had upset him, but I doubted it. My thinking said it was the presence of Gertrude and her meanness that had my boy in a case of nerves.

"You need to eat. You're as scrawny as a toothless man eating chicken necks." I yanked on a chair and pointed at the seat. "Sit. I'll get you something." As I traveled the path to the buffet, Sue Mie pushed in a little woman in a wheelchair, and a man in a walker followed them. I sent her a nod.

"It's almost quitting time for you."

She pushed the woman up to a table and motioned a cafeteria attendant over, probably to get their food. Sue helped the man in the walker into a chair then scooted the man's walker back a little and pushed his chair in. "I not be here for you, Mr. Gerber." Sue directed his line of vision to the smiling attendant headed their way. "Miss Nancy will help. I see you tomorrow."

Ah. She was keeping up the charade of Asian CNA. When she turned and our gazes connected, I knew the time had come for me to eat humble pie. "Sure could use me a nice hot mocha. Got any place around here that serves them?"

Whatever she was thinking, she hid it well. Too

well for my liking, but I had no choice.

"Coffeehouse down street. They close 6 p.m."

When, in fact, they closed at 9 p.m. Translation: Meet me there at 6 p.m.

"Sounds good. I'll try it."

I left her and went over to the buffet, helping myself, glad to be finished with the hard part of the humbling. I spooned up a pile of potatoes and a nice chunk of meat loaf, drowning it all in gravy. Canned, if I didn't miss my guess. I know fake food when I see it.

When I turned, two plates in hand, my eyes swept the room for Sue Mie. She'd already left, but then it was past five o'clock.

I set Darren's plate in front of him. He lifted his eyes to me without lifting his head. "Thank you."

He picked up his fork and rolled a green bean around in some gravy before nibbling at it. I admired the fact that he managed the fork quite well despite his tight hands.

Gertrude came up for air long enough from her monologue with Thomas to stab her meat loaf–laden fork at Darren. "Why don't you tell us what you think about Polly's fall, Darren? Everyone knows how much you didn't like her."

Darren about choked on a piece of food. His eyes rolled to me. Pleading. Though I wasn't sure what he was pleading for.

"Can't imagine Darren not liking anyone," Matilda offered. "He's a good boy."

Gertie wiped her mouth. "We need to keep an open mind, right, LaTisha? Isn't that what you're trying to do, make sure the whole incident was, indeed, an accident.

Why even the most innocent could be guilty."

We should be talking about you, then. But I realized it wasn't doing me any good to be thinking those words. "You got something to say about Polly? Being how you're so hard after Thomas, I'm guessing Polly put a curdle on your plans."

Thomas had the good grace to look only slightly bemused by my straight talk.

Gertrude huffed. "I would never have hurt Polly. She was my friend."

"You sure look mighty comfortable with her being cold."

Gertrude's eyes slipped over Darren then quick back to Thomas. She patted her beau's leg. "Thomas tried to placate the old dear by giving Polly the attention she so craved."

Another strained smile from Thomas. This man looked like he needed some Metamucil sprinkled on his beans.

"Seems to me Polly isn't the only one craving attention," Matilda jibed.

Gertrude's lips tightened. "Thomas and I plan on marrying."

Those words stunned us all into silence. Matilda was the first to recover. She laid her napkin on her plate. "His idea or yours?"

Gertrude's lips tightened even more, and her glance at Thomas practically screamed at him to say something. He sat placidly, the only sign of discomfort the sudden way he pushed his plate away. "We need to talk, Gertrude."

He stood, ramrod straight, and made straight for

the exit. Gertrude rolled upward and scrambled after him as fast as a locomotive could navigate an obstacle course of tables and chairs. Not that I have room to talk.

Darren sat stock still. "You made her real mad. She won't forget that." He was looking at Matilda, but I figured his words were for both of us.

"You think I'm caring about making her mad?" Matilda got to her feet with ease and braced herself against her cane, her gaze resting on Darren. "You don't let others tread you down, boy. You hear me?"

"I'm much better at defending others," he replied.

Something clicked in my mind. *Mitzi.* "Gertrude give Mitzi a hard time?"

"Sometimes. Mitzi loved her though. Loves her, I mean. I think it's me Gertrude doesn't care for. Not now anyway." He wouldn't quite meet my eyes.

"Time for you to be talking to me, Darren."

He let out his breath in a *whoosh*, his eyes cruising around us to make sure no one was nearby. "I saw Polly in Thomas's room the day she died. Saw your mother-in-law go into Thomas's room by mistake. Polly was real shocked when she saw Matilda, but she had a key to Thomas's apartment, so I wasn't too surprised to see her in there."

Not much that I didn't know. By the looks of him, there was something else he needed to get off his chest. I waited as patiently as a three-year-old. If he wasn't going to talk, I'd shake it out of him.

He took a long drink. "Polly told a couple of the residents about getting a threatening note. Everything made sense then. You see, I'd gone up to visit Mitzi one day and saw Gertrude sliding something under Polly's door."

Gertrude!

So the little love triangle was hairier than idle gossip.

I watched Darren hard for a minute, my mind clicking along. If this man knew love, he knew how to see it in others. "Thomas is a strange one."

"He's a good guy. He helps me keep an eye on Mitzi."

That at least explained why he had a key to Mitzi's apartment. "Do you think Thomas loves Gertie?"

Darren's dark eyes latched onto mine. "No. I think he loved Polly."

30

When I headed for the Nuthouse, I decided to take my cell phone with me in case Lela called. She would be arriving in Maple Gap anytime, and I wanted to hear how her visit with Sara went. I also needed to update her on our break-in, to put her mind at ease, even though Sara had the more important problem right now.

I turned my cell on and slipped it into my pocket. It did some beeping, which I ignored, until it buzzed real hard as I made my way out the front doors of Bridgeton Towers. The vibration of the phone in the pocket of my skirt sent every bit of cellulite on my right thigh into a frenzy. I dug it out, reading the caller ID before answering.

"Lela, girl, you back in Maple Gap?"

"Sure am, Momma. Got in later than I wanted. There's a message here from Chief Conrad saying something about the lab guy needs to know what he's looking for on the T-shirt. He forgot to ask. That make sense to you?"

It did. I was afraid of that. No way was Lab Guy going to know what to look for if I didn't narrow the field for him. This wasn't what I wanted to hear at all.

"You get to see Sara yet?"

Silence. "Yeah. She's so pale."

I heard the tightness in her voice. Even my own started to tightening. "Her momma and I had us a good talk. You'll cook for them for me, won't you, babe?"

"Sure thing. How's Grandma?"

We talked during my walk to the Nuthouse, with me reminding Lela that her stay at our house was temporary and she needed to get her résumés out there, as well as an update on last night's break-in. I assured her the thing was related to a case I was on, which alarmed her even more. I did my best to help her see that Matilda wasn't in immediate danger and poked at the fact that her visit home was going to be short. Right?

I'd already done empty-nest syndrome once; no way was I going to start taking chicks back into the nest when life slammed them. I'd worked hard to get used to having a hollow house, and the only thing I was after now was grandbabies. I made sure to remind Lela of that, too, before we hung up.

My phone jingled again. Once. I checked it and found a voice mail. From Chief Conrad. It was the same message Lela had just given me, so I deleted it as I stepped inside the Nuthouse, the cool air and coffee scent swirling around me.

Sue Mie sat in the same booth we'd talked in on our last visit, and bless her, she had another one of those marvelous mochas waiting for me.

She even pulled the table toward her before I began the task of wedging myself into the slot. "Least you could have done is got us a decent table. Not everyone's so skinny they can turn sideways and disappear."

Sue Mie slurped her cup of iced stuff and smiled. "I'm glad you came."

I managed to crack a smile myself. "You going to share with me or not?"

"I was hired by Thomas Philcher."

Whatever I expected, it wasn't that.

"Specifically to look into the background of Polly Dent."

"Did she suspect you were looking into her past?"

Sue Mie shook her head. "I don't think so. Most of detective work is keeping your ears open and your mouth shut."

How true.

I was glad to pull out the facts I already knew and wave them around a bit. "She's the ex-wife of Thomas's partner in his bank-robbing days."

"True. Manny Wilkins was the one to help me with that fact."

Me, too, but I wasn't saying it out loud. "Does Thomas know about her?"

"He does now, and it's one of the reasons I asked you here."

My brain was smoking. Darren's voice telling me just a few moments ago that he thought Thomas really loved Polly. . . If he found out she was the ex-wife of his partner after he had told her about the money, taking her into his confidence, he'd be livid. I would. "When did Thomas find out Polly's ex was his partner?"

"The day before Polly died in the gym accident."

I picked up my mocha and took a big gulp. "That's not looking too good for him." I was thinking *motive*.

It niggled at me to tell her about Gertrude's role in the whole thing. Still, nothing explained how Polly got into the gym that evening. I just couldn't see Thomas or Gertrude letting her in. "You got any ideas on how Polly got herself into that gym? I was thinking maybe she had a key made for herself."

"It would be hard for a resident to get a key, take it to have it copied, and get it back without the person missing it. You're talking a good span of time." Sue spread her hands. "Maybe someone left it unlocked for her?"

"Doubt it. She came into the cafeteria and made a scene to Otis. He left with her. I looked into that. Hilda Broumhild said he came right back."

"I discovered that Polly did have quite the reputation as an exercise enthusiast. She made frequent use of the gym. Maybe she and Otis had a quiet agreement on the side, and he let her go in without supervision."

"Still doesn't make sense. He'd be downright foolish risking his job like that."

Sue drained her cup dry. I gulped on my mocha a bit, thoughts swirling around enough to make me dizzy.

One thing stood out above all else. I still needed to have a look at those maintenance records for the treadmills. If I couldn't find Otis to help me get those records, surely his secretary would know where they were kept. Or Chester. Gave me indigestion just thinking about asking him for anything, but checking out that treadmill might give me a clue as to what to have the lab guy look for on the handlebars.

"I got a sample of the powder on the handles of the treadmill Polly fell off of and sent it to someone to analyze."

Sue's eyes went huge. "You don't think something was in the cornstarch stuff they use?"

"It was my husband's idea that it could be something besides baby powder." I saw no good reason to let her know Mitzi had been spouting poems to me. She probably wouldn't believe Mitzi could have seen something anyhow. "Found powder stuff all over the floor and even in. . ."

A lightbulb popped in my head.

Sue Mie's lips were moving, as if she hadn't heard me at all. "The treadmills had been switched. Mitzi's rhyme seemed to say that."

And here I thought I was the only one Mitzi spouted those poems to. It gave me a nice boost of courage, though, to think Sue Mie thought Mitzi's poems might be meaning something.

She kept on talking. "I'm guessing that Mitzi saw the person dragging the treadmill through that back hallway onto the elevator. It would make sense. He or she wouldn't be seen that way."

Hallway? "You saying that door by that service elevator is a hallway?"

"Sure, it runs from Otis Payne's office and behind the gym. It even has a bathroom, which I think is Mr. Payne's private domain, although I'm sure his secretary uses it as well."

"You ever check out that hallway after Polly's fall?"

Sue's eyes flashed a question. "I really hadn't thought of that. I just saw it as a way for someone covering a crime to get the treadmill out of there without having to use the front entrance to the gym."

"You have a key to it?"

"No, but I'm sure Mr. Payne or his secretary or a cleaning person would."

I had to look in on that hallway real soon.

Sue Mie tapped her chin. "When I saw that treadmill in the storage room, I was sure Mitzi was right."

"Chester let you in there?"

"He was one of the reasons I felt like Mitzi's poem really meant something. Chester told me I had to sign out anything I took from the storage room. Mr. Payne's orders."

"Hmph."

Sue nodded. "I'd never heard of that rule before, and I've been into the storage area plenty of times."

Maybe she was onto something, but I'd better get out what had gone through my head a minute ago, before Sue's talking made me forget. "That powder stuff we just talking about. It was in the trash can the day Otis let me into the gym to examine Polly."

She wasn't following me. I could just tell by the look on her face.

"Meaning someone dumped the powder in the trash," I added.

"Maybe they do that every night."

I didn't want to admit defeat here, but Sue Mie was pulling me down.

"What if we're wrong about all this?" she asked.

"Then, honey, we're gonna be rolling the crust, putting in the filling, and eating humble pie."

───

We decided Sue Mie was going to look into Polly's health records and find out what prescriptions she'd been on. The maintenance records were mine to investigate. We were set to compare notes the following evening at the Nuthouse.

Hardy and I rounded up our group of singers and had quite a choir going on in the main common area for a good while. We sang song after song, with seven sopranos, three altos, a couple of men who did decent tenors, and two basses who knew their stuff. At one point, even the nighttime staff got in on the action. Chester came by, a scowl on his face, dragging a trash bag.

"Singing's good for the soul." I beamed good nature and love. "Join us."

"I'm doing my job. Got trash to take out for tomorrow's pickup," he said, the expression he directed at the other two cleaning ladies who'd joined us minutes before clearly relaying the message that they were being lazy.

"You leave these ladies alone. They were hard at work and will be again after a while. Might as well enjoy themselves a few minutes."

Chester glared hard at me. I lasered him right back.

He rustled his bag and punched the elevator button, his back to me as he waited.

Singing was good for those who *had* a soul. Chester left me wondering. *Lord, forgive me.*

Hardy sent me a tired look that let me know the bed was calling him, so I wrapped up our night with "Battle Hymn of the Republic." Might as well stir some patriotism.

Sally and Mary were among the half dozen of us left at that point. I thought we'd lose them completely for the last song as they fussed over a small man in a wheelchair. The redheaded nurse who'd helped Manny Wilkins in the library the other day stood close to the man's side. On occasion the man would grimace, but he waved off the nurse when she tried to help. Sally and Mary both tried to help him, too, but he shook his head hard.

He seemed to settle down after a while, and Mary, following Sally's example, got back into the song until the last note died away and Hardy stood up. We all broke out and applauded one another. A low moan turned heads in the direction of the man in the wheelchair. Mary leaned over him as he desperately pressed a button connected to the arm of his wheelchair.

I made tracks toward them. Nurse Ane leaned over the man. "George? You still in pain?"

Sally leaned toward me. "Mr. Hendricks has terminal cancer."

My heart fell to my feet, my thoughts turning to our little Sara.

The nurse spoke with Mr. Hendricks for a while, then she put in her own call before she wheeled Mr. Hendricks in the direction of the nursing unit.

Sally comforted a teary Mary as they headed toward the elevators. So much sorrow.

Beside me, Hardy yawned and gave a gentle tug on my hand. "You wanting to go play Eskimo with me?"

I glanced at the wall clock, suprised to find it was only eight thirty. "A little early yet. Momma went up with Darren. Why don't you go check on her?"

"You trying to get rid of me?" He pouted.

Maybe it was the caffeine from the mocha making me suddenly restless. Sue might have forgotten to order me decaf. "I got to think."

"I'm not so tired I can't think with you."

"You just got through yawning big enough to

swallow a turkey whole, and you're telling me you're not tired?"

"Some, but as long as we're moving around, I'll stay awake." He held out his hand to me. "Come on, and let's take a walk."

"You're forgetting I already hauled myself down to that coffee shop. If I walk anymore, the friction from my thighs is gonna catch me on fire."

He wagged his eyebrows. "Then we'll find us a spot to stop and rest."

I knew what he was thinking. "We're a little old to be caught making out on a park bench."

His eyes glittered at me. "We're all legal-like to do it."

"You're like a snake weaving at me back and forth, trying out your charms."

"Hoping my best gal will relax and have some fun."

He gave one last tug on my hand that sent my reluctant feet into motion. He pulled me along, giving me a good view of his scrawny form and hiked britches. I grinned. He was as cute as a lop-eared bunny.

I hadn't given one thought to the cool breeze in the evening air on my way to meet Sue Mie, my mind overloaded with this mystery. Hardy was right: I needed to relax a bit, and every now and again, I let him be right.

We walked hand in hand for a while on the sidewalks that led around Bridgeton Towers. Each breath of the breeze on my skin made me grateful he'd brought me on the walk, and I tucked him closer under my arm.

"You still thinking on that restaurant?"

He nodded. "Yup."

"We'd make a good pair."

"Have made one for all these years."

"What about visiting our grandchildren? Can't do that and own a restaurant."

"Might have to hire someone extra."

We didn't talk for a while. Hardy slid out from under my arm and grabbed my hand again, walking faster. It took me a minute to see what had him in high gear. A bench. Straight ahead. One-track mind.

The night breezes stirred as he steamrolled us toward the seat. My nose caught a whiff of something bad. Hardy stopped stock-still, head cocked, sniffing the air like a bloodhound.

"Coming from over there." A white fence cordoned off an area connected to Bridgeton Towers; a little driveway led away from it and disappeared behind the building.

"Here I thought it was you," I said.

He bared his tooth. "Not this time." He wagged his hind end down on the seat and put his arm along the back of the bench. Whatever had gotten into him, I needed to make good and sure to shake it out of him. He was wearing me out with all that energy.

I didn't get the chance to sit down though. A scraping sound caught my ears, along with a flow of words not fit to repeat. The sound died. Then it started again, accompanied by another string of bad vocabulary. Hardy was looking in the direction of the fence.

"What do you think's going on?"

Hardy hiked himself up and ran over to the locked

door along the fence. "Need any help in there?"

"Get out of here."

Voice sounded mighty cranky but familiar. Chester's voice. What was he doing?

Not another sound came from the other side of the fence, and the boards were alternated to make it hard to see through, especially with night coming on.

I put my fingers to my lips and pointed up then cupped my hands. Hardy's face broke into a huge grin, but he shook his head. Then he faced the fence, hand working its way into his back pocket, slow but as sure as it could with his pants so tight. He withdrew a pocketknife, unfolded the blade, and made his way real slow-like down the length of the fence, studying it real hard.

When he began digging at a place in one of the boards, I understood. The knot popped out into his hand, and he glued his eye to the new peephole. For a long time. Too long, to my way of thinking. I finally tapped on his shoulder and scowled my impatience at him. He returned his eye to the hole for only a second, then he wedged the knot back into place, grabbed my hand, and hustled me away from the fence.

31

I t had better be good. *Real* good."

Hardy did a little happy dance in front of the recliner in Matilda's apartment, where I sat recovering from our dash back to Momma's room. If the chair hadn't felt so good and my legs not burned quite so badly, I might have made it into the bedroom. Without him. And locked the door. That'd teach him.

He perched on the arm of my chair, practically shaking with excitement. "Old Chester looked scared. He was standing out there, probably waiting to make sure we were good and gone before he continued what he was doing."

He paused, that tormenting look coming over his face.

I frowned hard, ready to give him a good tongue-lashing, when Matilda's bedroom door creaked open.

"You giving my daughter-in-law trouble, Hardy Barnhart?"

Now how'd she know that? "Did we wake you up, Momma?"

Her cane pounded the floor as she stumped over to the small sofa and sagged down into it. "Couldn't sleep. Then I heard you two and knew Hardy was making mischief."

It's one of the reasons I love her so much. She thinks like I do and smells trouble a mile away. I thought my intuition was sharpened by having raised seven babies, but Matilda was proof it took only one child to hone a momma to razor sharp.

Hardy slunk over to the sofa and took up residence next to her. Matilda patted his cheek. "Now you be a good boy and start talking."

"Fast," I added.

He leaned forward. I braced myself, waiting for the rip of material that announced the seam of his pants had done and given up the ghost. Nothing. Must be the polyester.

"It was the treadmill. All that screeching was the treadmill being pushed along the concrete."

"What treadmill?" This from Momma.

Hardy explained about the treadmill swap we suspected, while I made some mental notes. Sue Mie would be able to get into that storage room better than I could. I'd have to get a message for her to look and see if the treadmill was still there or not. I also wanted to know if it was normal for them to dump the platter of baby powder into the trash every night.

<hr>

Sue Mie put me right on the trail the next morning. Since it was only eight o'clock, I'd remained in my robe, stirred myself up a mocha, and put my mind to the mystery. So much still to do.

My cell phone rang, and Sue Mie's voice whispered across the line. She'd come in early to sneak a peek at Polly's records and found one major thing. Heart problems. Suspected heart attack and prescribed Digitran about two months previous. High cholesterol. She weighed a hundred pounds and was five feet seven inches.

"Any form of digoxin can be fatal if the dosage isn't right." Her whispers became frantic. "I only had a glimpse of things before a nurse came in. Tell your lab guy to look for digitalis. I'm working on getting you a key to that storage room, too. We'll meet tonight."

Digitran. Digoxin. Digitalis. Foxglove? I needed a computer. . .the Internet. . .a library. . .somewhere to research all this.

I made the call to Chief Conrad so he could relay the message about Polly's heart condition, but his reply didn't encourage me any.

"I can tell him, but you know this is going to take some time, don't you, LaTisha?"

"You sayin' more than twenty-four hours?"

"Probably more like a week, tops. If you don't have that much time, you should look it up on the Internet or see if you can find some books in a library on poisons."

I snapped my cell phone shut after asking about Chief's wife, stuffing down my disappointment. A week. Tops. *Lord, I need some help here.*

Hardy must have slid his heels to the floor, because next thing I knew, he was padding over to me, looking all warm and tousled in his pajamas and stocking feet. "You looking a little crazy there."

"Lots going on." And as much as I wanted to go down to the library, I also needed to poke around a bit more, maybe visit Mitzi Mullins and see if she had any more poetry.

Hardy stretched out in a chair beside me, hands across his belly. The picture of contentment. I stared down at his toes, wiggling happily in his thick white socks to the tune of some song he had stirring in his head.

"What you think you're doing?"

One eye popped open. "Enjoying the moment."

I huffed. "We need to get moving. Lots to do today."

"You first."

"Where's Momma?"

Hardy's toes stopped dancing. "Probably sleeping late after last night."

"She'll miss breakfast."

"No, she won't. I'll make sure of it." He closed his eyes again. "Heard from Lela?"

"She called yesterday, told me she'd visited Sara."

Hardy's answer was to slide his hand across to mine and grab it tight. "What you flapping at me for?"

I puffed out a breath. I squeezed his hand. "Guess I owe you a pie, huh?"

His eyes crinkled at me. "I'm losing count. Now talk."

I was worried about the whole Polly Dent thing. Thomas, Gertrude, Dr. Kwan, Sue Mie, Otis and Louise Payne. . . "I want to go home." And that was the naked truth.

"Um-hm."

"I miss being there."

He rolled his eyes at me. "What else is going through that mind of yours?"

I closed my eyes tight, lower lip quivering, busted wide open by his simple statement. He read me so well. "What if the doctor says what I don't want to hear?"

"You'll deal with it. Same as you taught our babies.

'Life happens—get used to it.' "

"You'd be happy to hear I'm dying?"

"Naw. But seeing as only the good die young, I've got nothing to worry over."

I reached out and touched him on that one. He sat up straight and rubbed his shoulder, playing the injured innocent, all the while his expression full of pure badness.

"Well if that's so, the Good Lord won't be issuing you an invitation either."

"Compassion gets me in." He nodded. "He's loving me for loving you when no one else would."

"Well, love me enough to get yourself down to the library and research digoxin."

He screwed his mouth up. "Did you just cuss?"

"Di-gox-in. It's a poison from the foxglove plant."

"Why not just ask a nurse or a doctor?"

I pushed myself up from the sofa. "If I was wanting everyone to know what I was doing, I would."

"You want research." He hopped to his feet and saluted me. "I'm your man."

"You sure are, baby. You sure are."

32

First thing I wondered was whether Otis Payne worked on Saturdays. I was sure his secretary didn't. I wouldn't be doing overtime. Being married was secretary duty enough for me. Truth be told, secretaries are nothing more than babysitters. Which is one of the reasons I'd lambasted Lela when she quit college for her "dream job" of being assistant to someone else. But I got to let her grow up and learn the hard way.

But stewing over Lela wasn't going to get me those maintenance records any sooner.

I skimmed a hand over my hair, balling it up in a clip until I could get back to Maple Gap and Regina's magical fingers on my scalp.

I slid one of my favorite dresses over my head and rooted around in our suitcase for a new pack of pantyhose. Brought along a few spares in case I got to walking and my legs got to rubbing so much that my body overheated and the nylon stuck to my skin.

I snapped the waistband of my sky blue dress into place. None of those stiff, unforgiving, nonelasticized waistbands for me. I needed my dress to expand and contract on cue.

As I was headed out, Hardy came into our bedroom all fresh and dewy from the shower and wrapped in his robe with a lemon yellow towel on his head. "You're looking wider than the great blue sky."

I smoked him with my eyes. "And you're looking

like lemon soft serve with that towel on your head."

"Sweet as an ice-cream cone."

I snorted and looked down at the floor. "Well, Mr. Ice-Cream Cone, you're dripping."

I left Hardy mopping up his mess and began mapping out my mission. First off, find out where those maintenance records were kept. Second, investigate that back hallway if I could figure out a way to get into it. I'd stop in for a visit with Mitzi Mullins on the way, since she was on this floor.

I wasn't too surprised to find Darren with Mitzi, but the fact that she answered the door made my heart swell with excitement for Darren. The boy beamed at me, a book spread in his lap. Mitzi didn't say a word but went straight over to the empty chair next to Darren and sat down.

"Back in operation." I beamed back at him.

"She's really good." Darren handed the book over to Mitzi, who held it for him, though she didn't seem lucid enough to really know what she had.

Darren glanced at Mitzi, who toyed with the material covering the armrest, then back at me. He seemed to be hoping for her to say something, his smile wilting when Mitzi remained quiet.

Darren got to his feet and motioned me to follow him. I wondered what the boy was up to. He led me into Mitzi's room and to the dresser that held her medication bottles.

His bent fingers uncurled to grab one of the bottles. "When I came to see Mitzi yesterday, I noticed a new prescription bottle, same as the old one." He held both up for me to see. "It seemed strange for Dr. Kwan to give her another one when the old bottle still had capsules, so I did my own little investigation."

I watched as he popped the lid on the old prescription bottle and emptied out the contents onto the dresser. Capsules, broken in two. Empty.

"She's supposed to take one of these a day, and I'm sure she was, but empty capsules don't help anyone."

"The new bottle has full capsules?" I asked even as I took the new prescription from him and unscrewed the cap. Sure enough, these capsules were all full.

"Pills and bottles all in a row, Polly knew about the foe."

At the sound of the voice, Darren and I turned quick-like. Mitzi stood in the doorway.

He went to her and put his hand on her arm. "Why don't you sit back down?"

She looked past him though, eyes on me. "Missus knows his secret and will hide it, too, if only the subject will remain taboo."

My mind churned around the possibilities as Darren patted Mitzi's arm. "Who is 'Missus'?"

"Life isn't all love and fame; some of it is filled with pain."

Darren didn't seem to know what to think, but I sure had a mind full. Her first line was revealing. Polly knew about the pills and bottles and about the "foe."

"Who did you see, Mitzi?" I asked, hoping she'd reveal more. "Who is it you want me to catch?"

Mitzi didn't even flinch. "I need to go to the bathroom."

—

I crept around the part of the first floor open to the

assisted-living residents, waiting for something to jump out at me. A lady sat at the front desk. Normal. The library was open, but the posted sign indicated closing time on Saturdays as noon. Hardy was nowhere to be seen. I glanced at the clock on the wall and found out he had exactly two hours to get his nose in a book before the doors locked. Maybe he'd gone to the library in town. I took the time to check the parking lot for Old Lou. The Buick sat in the same spot I'd left it.

Where was that man?

Someone tapped on my shoulder. "You missin' me already?"

I twisted around to face his grinning self. "What you doing, trying to scare me stiff?" Never mind how I managed to miss seeing him sneak up on me. He delighted in harassing me.

"You were stretching your neck awful hard at those elevators."

I pointed. "That library closes in two hours, and you haven't even slithered yourself into the place."

He withdrew his hand from behind his back and dangled a key in front of me. "Got me something better than a pile of books to read."

This man makes me crazy. "What you spoutin' off about?"

His voice got real quiet as he lowered his hand. "Sue Mie stopped by right after you left. Gave me the key, and I asked her about digoxin." His eyes shimmered. "It stimulates the ticker of heart patients. Can be poisonous in high doses."

"And you're gonna be telling me what that key is for."

His grin went huge. "A certain hallway she said you were interested in."

My heart took off beating real hard. The key to the back hallway! I held out my hand.

Hardy shook his head and pushed the key into his front pants pocket. "I'm wanting to go with you. This could be dangerous."

"You hand me that key, or I'm gonna yank your drawers up so high you'll be halfway to heaven."

He crossed his arms and shook his head. "Besides, I'm already half there when I'm with you."

"None of that sweet talk." I held out my hand. "You'd better cross my palm with that key."

"Now's that any way to talk to the man of your dreams?"

I tapped my index finger against my outstretched palm. "Take a deep breath. Smell those funeral flowers yet?"

Hardy's expression was mulish. Then his eyes went real wide at something behind me.

"Mr. and Mrs. Barnhart."

I shot a look over my shoulder at the approaching Otis Payne. He stroked a hand over his head, doing a little scratch that released a few flakes, then stuck out his hand.

Huh-uh.

No way was I gonna shake after seeing what I just saw.

Hardy got real close to me. "We was thinking about taking ourselves on a little walk. Our walk last night did some real good."

Otis Payne's hand kind of faded down to his side,

though something in those beady blue eyes seemed to go real cool, real fast. I'm guessing Chester had recognized Hardy's voice from the night before and probably reported to Otis. But an innocent man shouldn't have anything to worry about, right? Could be he was just miffed over us not shaking his head-scratching hand.

"Our grounds are quite lovely this time of year."

Hardy's head bobbed in agreement. "You got quite a nice little fence around your trash area."

I was sending out more signal strength than a cell phone tower at that moment, trying to get my boy to shut his mouth.

"Heard Chester out there cussing up a storm."

Otis got real still. Not that he was jumping around before, but something changed in his expression, and it wasn't making him any prettier.

I locked onto Hardy's hand and squeezed hard. "We need to be on our way now. You have a good day, Mr. Payne."

I headed Hardy around the corner of the library, past Otis's office and the gym, and pulled up tight at the service elevator. "What you doing spouting off about Chester? He was mad for sure."

Hardy ran a finger in his ear. "Flush him out. Sometimes you hold on to things too much. Let him know you saw something, and it'll make him do something."

"He was looking like he was going to skin us alive is what he looked like."

"Why would he feel that way if he weren't worried?"

Hardy truly had a point, as much as it pained me

to admit it. After Otis's assurance that the police didn't have any concerns regarding Polly's "accident," news that I was still poking around, still questioning things might stir him up a bit.

Without another word, I stretched out my hand again. Hardy fished out the key and slapped it into my palm. "Knowing Otis is here, this might not be a wise thing to be doing right now."

I sent him a searing look. "You just said it was time to stir things up."

"It's easy to say when I'm the one doing the stirring."

The key slid into the lock with a bit of pressure, telling me it was a new key. Sue Mie must have made a copy. I tried the knob of the door, and it twisted real easy, revealing a long hallway with a door at the end, one on the left, and one on the right, closer to where we stood. Quick mental aerobics let me know the door on the right had to lead to the gym area.

Hardy got to that door first, while I eased the one we'd just come through shut. No use having it slam and let everyone know we'd arrived.

Hardy did a little jig in front of the closed door. "Here they are! Here they are!"

"Quiet down there. This hallway connects to Otis's office and who knows what else. You want someone to catch you acting like a three-year-old?" But my maturity slipped hard, too, when I laid eyes on the papers tacked to the door. Maintenance records.

I flipped to page 2. The treadmills were listed by number.

T61 had been crossed out completely.

33

I hugged Hardy good and tight. "This has got to mean something," I whispered next to his ear. "Why else would they get rid of T61 right after Polly's fall?"

Hardy didn't say a word but turned and headed down the hallway to the next door. I wanted to know how this door led into the gym. I knew there wasn't another door visible. That's when those fingerprints on the glass mirrors popped a flash of light into my head. The door slid open easily, and sure enough, the other side was one of the mirrored glass panels, and exactly the one I saw with fingerprints all over it. So this door was used often. Obviously the maintenance guy knew of its existence.

Next thing I knew, Hardy was tapping me on the shoulder, eyes rolling around in his head like he'd done gone lunatic. "Someone's in Otis's office. They said your name."

I quick closed the mirrored door and hustled up the hallway. Hardy glued his ear to one spot low on the door, me to another spot higher up.

". . .tell her what you saw. . .right. . .good-bye."

Hardy frowned.

I straightened, disappointed I hadn't heard more. I pantomimed to Hardy to keep listening while I checked out the only door left we hadn't examined. He caught on to the meaning of my motions and stuck his ear against Otis's office door again.

I got the other door open real easy and flicked on

the light. A bathroom. It had to be the one Sue Mie had mentioned. It included a sink, toilet—seat in the salute position, obviously the work of a person of male persuasion—and a small, square shower with a plain dark green curtain.

My first act of business was to right a wrong. I seized a fistful of toilet paper and used it to grab the toilet seat and lower it. You treat a woman like a queen, then you prepare her throne—that's my motto and the reason I trained my boys to put it down when they finished. Not that they listened all the time. Several nights I had a chilling surprise, but they heard about it the next day and got latrine duty for a week.

I threw away my wad of paper instead of flushing it, not wanting to make any noise. I stuck my head into the shower and spied a bar of soap, a mirror, and razor. I was just closing the curtain when the door swung open behind me. I craned my neck that direction in time to see Hardy's eyes about bugging out of his head. He spread his arms wide and came at me, catching me and sending us both into the shower, almost yanking the curtain from its hooks.

"What you doing?"

He smashed his hand over my mouth. "Someone's coming."

He turned and stepped on my toe then rammed his bony elbow into my stomach. By the time I got knocked in the jaw with his head and took another stab in the stomach, I was ready to wash him down the drain. But Hardy's goal had been to turn around and pull the shower curtain shut. He eased it across the opening real slow.

We waited. The handle to turn on the water was sticking in my back, my dress twisted around, and our breathing was steaming up the shower mirror.

The door to the bathroom opened. I sucked in a breath. If whoever it was intended to use the toilet, my idea about the toilet seat might have been a real bad move. Too late now.

The seconds dragged. It ran through my mind that whoever it was better not be undressing to take a shower, because there was gonna be some serious company. Something creaked. Then I heard water in the sink. Something rattled. Another squeak. Shuffling. A dull thud.

I can tell you I wanted that door to open fast and this person to be making an exit before I exploded. The handle of the shower dug real hard in my back. I shifted. Bad idea. Water dribbled from the shower head onto my scalp and down my neck. Cold water. I swallowed a gasp and tried to shift back to my original position to turn off the water. It still dripped.

At long last, the door opened then closed.

Hardy and I stayed stock-still for a full minute before he peeked around the curtain. "They're gone."

I pushed on him to hustle him out. As soon as I had extra elbow room, I twisted the lever to OFF and stepped out, glad for room and fresh air. Now to figure out what our visitor had been up to. The toilet seat remained down, and we'd heard no flush. Over the sink, a medicine cabinet presented a possibility for creating a creaking noise. I opened it. It let out a nice low screech, the same as the one we'd heard. Inside were several bags of pills. Pink, blue, white. A container of empty capsules.

Hardy came up beside me and pointed to the trash can, where a prescription bottle and several capsules lay.

I motioned him to take the bag out of the trash can. I'd gone and took the stuff from the cabinet but was afraid it, as evidence, would mess up the chain of custody. That'd put a real hurting on the case. I'd take the trash and look at it real close for clues. Hardy tied a knot in the bag and held it out to me, Adam's apple bobbing hard. I patted his head and jabbed a finger at the door. It was time to make our escape.

Before Hardy got the door opened for me, I stuffed the stash down the front of my dress, shaping it just so, to look like it was part of me. A cup size bigger, maybe, but part of me.

Hardy lost his scared-stiff look, flashed his tooth at me, and swung the door wide.

34

We almost made it to the first-floor elevators. Almost. Dr. Kwan came out of the cafeteria as Hardy and I were trucking along.

"Mrs. Barnhart. I'd like to talk to you a moment."

Hardy slowed. I didn't.

"If you please. There is something I have not told you that I'd like you to look into for me regarding Polly Dent."

I stopped dead. He wanted to talk about Polly? Wanted *me* to look into something? Having heard too much negativity about the man, I didn't trust him, but I wanted to hear what he had to say. Real bad.

I turned, trying to casually cross my arms over my chest, but managed only to scoot the bag out of alignment. Dr. Kwan's gaze never wavered from my face, as if he saw lopsided women all the time. Not that I expected him to ask about something so personal.

"I'd like to talk in private." He gestured across the hall like I didn't have any idea where Otis Payne's office was by now. "We can use Mr. Payne's office or his secretary's if he is too busy working."

"I didn't think doctors worked on Saturday. Don't they play golf or something?" This from Hardy.

"I was called in."

Since Otis Payne's secretary wasn't in and her door was locked, Otis's was open, something I hadn't noticed earlier. Maybe I was getting crazy in the head. Otis wasn't anywhere to be seen.

Dr. Kwan chose not to sit behind Otis's desk and instead chose an armchair. Hardy slouched on the sofa, and I stood. If I sat, the bag might make a crinkling sound. And the plastic was molded to me, making me sweat.

"Need to get myself upstairs real quick, got somethin' cookin'."

Hardy tilted his head. "No you don't."

"*Yes. I. Do.*" I emphasized so it'd get through Hardy's thick head to keep his mouth shut. And something sure was cooking. *Me.* Getting upstairs and shucking this bag would make me real happy-like.

"I won't take long, Mrs. Barnhart. Something has been troubling me about the day Polly died. I didn't mention it to the police because, well, I couldn't imagine Mr. Philcher doing anything untoward, but now. . ." He crossed his legs and clasped his hands over his knee. "You see, I saw Mr. Philcher go into the gym that day. Mrs. Dent had an appointment with me to be evaluated, though she was early. I heard her and Mr. Philcher fighting over something—"

"You telling me *you* let her into the gym?"

He made a face. "Actually, no. Mr. Payne let her in so she could prepare for the evaluation. She had heart problems, you see—"

"The police know all this?"

"I did mention Polly's evaluation to them, yes, but not the part about seeing Mr. Philcher. As I said, I couldn't believe he might be the vindictive type."

Uh-huh. "No one was supposed to be in that gym after hours unsupervised."

"A mere miscommunication. Mr. Payne didn't get

my message to have an attendant there. The police understood the problem and recognized it."

"Sounds like a lawsuit waiting to write itself," I said.

"Yes, we regret the mistake and will cooperate fully with the joint committee's investigation of the matter, but what I wanted to ask is if Mr. Philcher had mentioned his argument with Mrs. Dent that evening."

"Not to me." But I'd be sure to ask Thomas about it. If still water truly did run deep, then Thomas's temper might have gotten the better of him that night. If he'd been worried enough about Polly's intentions to hire a private investigator to have her checked out. . .

Dr. Kwan uncrossed his legs and rasped his palms together. "Thank you for your time, Mrs. Barnhart. I think I'll need to report this after all."

"I don't trust him," I huffed at Hardy as we continued up the stairs to the second floor. Well, as *I* continued up; he was already at the top. Whistling a tune. "If my legs weren't shaking so—" Pant. Pant. "I'd bound up these steps, too."

Hardy struck a pose. "Goes to show you what fine shape I'm in."

Two more steps.

"I'm gonna shape you"—pause, breathe—"into a ball and bounce you"—gasp, breathe—"down these steps if you don't stop your"—in with the good air, out with the bad air—"foolishness."

I planted both feet on the landing. "I don't care.

How long it takes. To wait for the elevator. Next time, I'll wait." It had been Hardy's idea to skip the elevator when we saw the lunch crowd waiting to stampede onto it once it landed on the first floor.

His eyebrows about touched his hairline as he peered up at me. "Why don't you trust Dr. Kwan?"

It took me a minute to remember our original conversation when we'd started up the steps. Why didn't I trust Dr. Kwan? Because he'd never condescended to give us much time before today. Because the residents didn't have much nice to say about him. Because things didn't feel right.

"You think he's making up what he said about Thomas?" Hardy asked.

With my heart rate down to a slow trot, I rallied enough to get through the door Hardy held and then down the hall. I'd never been so glad to see Matilda's apartment, especially her recliner, up close and personal.

But Matilda was in it.

I detoured toward the sofa and took a load off, my mind split between my heart rate, my thirst, and peeling the hot plastic bag from my chest. I made short work of the plastic bag, opening it up on my lap so Hardy could see the contents.

"What you two been up to?" Matilda asked, looking over her reading glasses at us. I could see she was halfway through the crossword puzzle of the paper.

"We went exploring, Momma." Hardy pointed at the bag I held.

I shook around the bag without touching the bottle, knowing I'd mar fingerprints if I did. Hardy adjusted the floor lamp so we could see better. I gasped as the label came into view. It was Mitzi Mullins's old prescription bottle. The lid was off, and the capsules that had been broken open upstairs on her dresser must have been the same ones we were laying our eyes on right then.

Hardy and I eyeballed each other. "Whoever was in that bathroom must have remembered the old prescription bottle and gone back to get it."

"Too late though," I said, feeling smug. "We saw it first."

"You got yourself some clue or something?" This from Matilda.

"Looks an awful lot like someone is stealing prescription drugs," I offered, setting aside the bag.

She set down her paper and pen. "You'll get them, LaTisha. You and my boy. You two eat yet?"

"No, ma'am," Hardy answered her. "I'll go down to the cafeteria with you. Some of the lunch crowd is already finished, so we shouldn't have to wait long."

Matilda tugged off her reading glasses. "Never you mind. That nice man next door is taking me down."

Hardy and I exchanged a look before he asked, "You mean Thomas?"

"Won't Gertrude be mad?" I asked.

She placed her glasses on the side table and made to rise. Hardy gave her a hand up. "He's not worried about her." She smoothed her hair and straightened her purple blouse. "He is a charmer. And no, I haven't lost my head over him, neither. I'm too old for that nonsense. At my age I can afford to flirt a bit and have some fun without anyone thinking I'm easy."

Someone knocked on the door. Matilda glanced

at the wall clock. "He's right on time. Get that for me, Hardy. I need to go." She slipped into the bathroom and shut the door as Hardy greeted Thomas.

Thomas.

He was right here.

And I was ready.

But his next action put time into real slow motion. Thomas showed me his grillwork, then he reached a hand into his pocket and pulled out a silver-wrapped candy, peeled off the foil, and popped it into his mouth.

Hardy clapped him on the back, you know, like men do to each other. Makes me think their tonsils might fly out their mouths. Anyhow, Thomas headed my way. I got vertical and leaned in toward him as he greeted me.

"Good to see you again—"

That's all he got out before I inhaled deeply right in his face. "You sure are minty fresh."

He withdrew his hand but laughed out loud. "My favorite flavor has always been mint."

"You take some wherever you go?"

"Well, yes." He got a strange look on his face.

"Can I have one?"

His movements were a little more deliberate as he reached into his breast pocket and withdrew a candy. I caught Hardy's eye where he hung over Thomas's shoulder, eyes huge, like he was witnessing the cheese slipping off my cracker.

As soon as that little silver wrapper made contact with the palm of my hand, I knew. Dr. Kwan had been right. I untwisted the wrapper and popped the mint into my mouth, examining the wrapper as excitement built in my chest.

I speared Thomas hard with my eyes. "You know" —I held up the wrapper—"I found one of these by Polly's treadmill after she fell. You have anything to say on that?" I figured I'd lead him to the confessional but wouldn't force him inside. If he didn't want to come clean, I'd push a little harder. But I think he saw something in my face.

We stood eyeball-to-eyeball for a full minute before Matilda's return from the bathroom jarred us out of our standoff.

"I'm ready now, Thomas," Matilda said, still rubbing her hands together from putting on the lotion she always used after washing up.

Thomas backed down first, seeming to collapse into himself a bit. He stared at his hands as if he saw something we didn't, and I readied myself for the confession of a killer.

35

"I t's not what you might think" were the last words out of Thomas's mouth before he buried his face in his hands and started sobbing.

"What's going on?" Matilda asked.

Hardy went over to his momma and patted her back, whispering something into her ear and steering her into her recliner before returning to Thomas's side. His other side. Hardy was placing himself between Thomas and the front door in case he made a run for it. My man's mind is sharp as a razor; not that I thought his scrawny body could bring Thomas down, but he could certainly present an obstacle to slow progress until I could body slam him.

Thomas's rivers finally dried up, and he accepted a tissue I'd yanked from the box next to the sofa. He sank down onto the sofa and braced his hands on his knees, head down. "Polly was a good woman. I—I loved her so much. I trusted her. She wanted this apartment so we could be close." His hand clenched around the tissue. "All those years I spent in jail and ached to be free, to start over and be a good citizen seemed within reach when I came here. I met Polly and thought she was everything I'd wanted—spunky, fun, maybe a little eccentric." He shrugged. "But who isn't at our age?"

"I'm guessing she didn't tell you about her ex."

"No." Another clenching of the tissue. "And when I found out, it was like she'd shot me. Deceived me. All I could think was how I'd been tricked and played for a fool. She wanted my money, and it seemed to become clear that her association with Otis Payne was for reasons less than honorable."

"You think they were looking for your stash?"

"*Stash* is too big a word." Thomas gave a little chuckle. "It's not much, you see, because I paid back everything I stole. But the small amount I had invested of my own money had grown to a nice sum, and I guess she thought there was more and that as my partner's ex she had a right to it."

"You didn't think so."

Thomas raised his head. "It wasn't about the money. I don't care about the money, but I knew others who might have found out my identity might show an interest in me because they thought I had money."

"You didn't want to be played for a fool," I said, straight out.

"The whole thing over the robberies was the foolish mistake of an immature mind. In that last note she left for me, it was as if the money meant so much to her. Not even she understood that it wasn't the money I stole with her ex, it was my own."

"But you were in the gym that day."

He closed his eyes and pulled in a deep breath of air. "She'd betrayed me. My trust. I was so angry."

"You found out after we saw you get off the elevator that day we first met?"

"Sue Mie is a private investigator just starting out. I'd hired her to look into Polly's background, just to make sure. . ." He massaged his forehead, and I understood how hard it must be for a wealthy person to trust in people's displays of love for him.

He sucked in air. "Sue Mie got the message to me right after Polly and I dined together that afternoon."

"So you got all mad and went down to have it out with her?"

"I saw Otis open the gym door for her. Watched as she powdered up and got ready to walk, Otis and her whispering the entire time. I hated it. Hated them. They were talking about the money. Plotting how they would split it, but more than that, I hated her deception. I watched Otis leave and would have gone in then to face her, but your husband was coming down the hall. He stopped and went into the gym."

"Polly said just a few things to me." Hardy nodded. "She was going back to Otis and demanding my momma be moved, but. . ." Hardy paused. "Right before I left, it was like she zoned out on me. She kept swallowing real hard."

"Why didn't you say that earlier?" I asked.

"I figured she was just mad or out of breath and wishing she had some water."

Thomas picked up the story again. "When your husband left, I went in. . .I can still see her face when I told her what I knew. She didn't care. Didn't even answer me. She just jabbed at the button to slow the machine down and wiped at her face."

Thomas ran a hand over his head and down his neck. "I've been over that scene so many times. Why did I pull the key? Why didn't I—"

"You pulled the key out?"

"She wouldn't answer me. Like she just didn't care about me, about what we had. I knew then that I hated her, and I pulled on the string of the emergency key where she had it clipped to her waist."

"She fell."

Thomas shook his head. "She stumbled and caught herself."

"She didn't scream or rage or yell?" That didn't sound like Polly, and I'd known her for only those few minutes.

Thomas's brow squeezed hard. "No. That's why I was so angry. It was like I didn't mean anything to her."

"You didn't find it strange?"

"I guess I didn't think about it until now. You think it meant something?"

"Did you see her fall?" I asked.

"No." Thomas leaned forward. "When I realized what I had done, how it could have hurt her and landed me back in jail again, I left."

Hardy stared hard at me, sending signals of some sort. "Dr. Kwan said he saw Thomas with Polly."

I cocked my head at him, wondering if he was percolating a full pot. "We know that."

Hardy moved closer to me. "Tish, Otis told us that evening after we found Polly that he *had to call Dr. Kwan in.*"

"Then how could he have seen. . ." I know my eyes must have bulged out of my head then. I recalled Darren's statement about Polly yelling at him. Polly's reputation was one of a fighter. Her words, her choice of weapon.

"Poison," Hardy said pure and simple. "It comes together."

"Digoxin?" I asked.

"Something laid her out." Hardy nodded.

Thomas cleared his throat. "You mean to tell me you think Polly was poisoned? But how?"

I asked a question of my own. "Mitzi's doing better. I was up there earlier, and Darren showed me something. She has a new bottle of prescription pills that she's been taking. Darren said he wondered why there was a new bottle when her old bottle wasn't yet finished. Since no one seems to trust Dr. Kwan, Darren checked the old prescription bottles. Those capsules were all empty. Just now, Hardy and I found some things in a bathroom behind the gym. Empty capsules and lots of pills in different colors."

Thomas looked stunned. "Is he stealing the drugs and replacing them with something else?"

My excitement built. "Polly never mentioned anything about Dr. Kwan? Anything strange?"

He pinched his eyebrows together. "The only thing I can think of was where she said in her note that certain people were desperate for money. Do you think she knew something about Dr. Kwan?"

Hardy crossed his arms. "If so, it sure gives him a motive to shut her up."

I had something to add to the pot now. "Sue Mie said Mitzi had told her the same rhymes she told me. If she told others and they thought she really had seen something that implicated them, it would be a good reason to keep her quiet."

"And what better way than to give her fake capsules of the drug she relies on for clarity?" Thomas added.

Matilda broke her silence, her back rigid, hands braced on her cane. "One thing you are all forgetting,

Sue Mie gave Polly a sugar snack instead of a sugar free. Did the same thing to me. What's to say that she didn't do Polly in?"

36

When my cell phone started ringing, we were all a little spooked. Caller ID showed Sue Mie was on the other end.

"LaTisha, listen, I've been looking around the building, trying to stay low. I found something I want you to see. Meet me in the basement."

"And why don't you just tell me over this here phone?"

"You won't believe what's down here. I need a witness."

Then she hung up. Okay. Right. Sue Mie wasn't one to talk in long stretches, but a good-bye would have been nice. And she'd sure be surprised when I didn't show up. This black woman doesn't do damp basements with mice and crawly things.

When Hardy found out what the phone call was about, he got to flapping like a momma hen over her chicks. "No way are you going there alone."

"You are so right."

Hardy stopped stomping long enough to cock his head at me. "You're not going at all?"

"Remember when Bryton was little and went down to the basement. Then he got all mulish on me?"

Hardy grinned and nodded. "You let him stay down there, 'cuz you had it made up that all the critters down there would teach him a good lesson."

"Did, too. Came screeching up those steps at first sight of a mouse. Slept with the lights on for a month after that. And that house he and Fredlynn just bought, it didn't have a basement, did it?"

"Mrs. Barnhart," Thomas piped up. "Why don't I go down there? I'll explain how you hate basements."

Now that didn't set well with me. Sending someone to do what I could do for myself. Too, I had to remember that Sue Mie might have something up her sleeve. But why? We were working together.

Hardy said it for me. "You have to go, LaTisha."

"I don't *have* to do anything, Hardy Barnhart."

"I'll go with you and protect you from the critters."

I pushed away the idea of cobwebs and mice. "If anything touches me, I'll scream so loud they'll think it's the fire alarm."

Thomas went with us to show us the way. Apparently the elevator didn't go to the basement. The going down was easy, but I sure dreaded hiking myself back up those stairs. Why did all this investigating involve exercise?

We made it all the way down to a lit hallway. Not too bad. "How'd you know where to find the basement?" I asked Thomas.

Thomas smiled. "Not much to do around here some days, so I explore, but the doors down here are usually locked." He pointed at the door straight ahead of us down a dimly lit, narrow hall. "I'll stay right here in case you need me."

Hardy followed me a good ways, when a humming sound caught our attention. A tiny room held two vending machines. I knew I'd lost Hardy completely. The one thing he can't pass up is a vending machine. I kept right on going as he gravitated to the things like a man who'd fasted for forty days and nights, his hand already working down into his pocket for some change.

I kept going, making sure to look through the little square window in the door. The room beyond didn't look too bad. It was well lit, and Sue Mie was clearly visible. She even waved me in.

The door slammed shut behind me, and I took two steps into that room when Sue Mie's smile flatlined.

"I'm sorry," she whispered, her head turning to the right in time for me to see Dr. Kwan step from behind some shelving. There was a prescription in his hand that had my name on it. He raised the gun and motioned me over next to where Sue Mie sagged in her chair, defeated.

"It's good to see you again, Mrs. Barnhart," Dr. Kwan said.

"You better stop waving that thing in my face."

"Somehow I don't think you're the one with the upper hand here. Now sit." He motioned to two chairs out of the line of the windows. I sat.

"Sue Mie did a good job getting you down here. Did you come alone?"

Good thing Thomas had stayed back a ways. I wondered, though, if they'd seen Hardy. Vending machines aren't the quietest things when they drop their selections. What if. . .

Dr. Kwan's eyes shifted away from Sue Mie and me, but that gun had its beady little eye on us all the same.

"Ah, Mr. Barnhart. Bring him over here next to these two, Otis."

My heart sank to my toes.

Hardy stood in front of Dr. Kwan and took a bite of a cheese puff like his swivel chair didn't turn full circle. "You boys shouldn't be pointing a gun at ladies."

Otis dragged a chair over from somewhere, and now he had a good length of nylon cord draped over one shoulder. He pointed at the seat. Hardy took his meaning, sat, and kept munching.

"I'll take those." Dr. Kwan held out his hand.

"Nothing comes between my man and his food," I warned. "You'd better back off when it comes to cheese puffs."

Dr. Kwan pointed his gun at my head. "This is not Comedy Central, Mrs. Barnhart, and you're not in control of this situation. I am." He turned back to Hardy and made a grab for the bag, just as Hardy threw the entire contents in Kwan's face.

Cheese puffs went up, and we all started going wild. Sue Mie and I rose as one. She knocked the gun from Dr. Kwan's hand with some kind of karate hi-ya move, while I pinned him with my size 24 body.

Sue Mie scooped up the gun and handed it to me. "Hold it on him."

I eased up on Dr. Kwan's gut and had his heart as my bull's-eye. I had my back to the action going on behind us, but I could hear muffled groans and grunts. I did my job and kept that gun pointed right at Dr. Kwan's chest as Sue Mie glanced that direction.

Her concerned look quickly turned into a chuckle

then an outright laugh. Dr. Kwan seemed to be following her line of thinking, because he looked like he was going to be sick.

"What's going on back there?" I asked.

Sue Mie grabbed one of Dr. Kwan's arms and pulled him from the wall, catching the other and bringing it behind his back, using the nylon cord to bind him. Only after she finished tying him to the chair did I relax my gun hand and turn to look behind me.

Matilda held her cane up like a weapon as Hardy and Thomas held Otis between them.

"Hurry up, Tish," Hardy said. "I'm hungry."

Epilogue

We're home now. I'm snuggled down in Maple Gap with a mocha in my hand, satisfied to have another solved mystery under my belt. Hardy is on the sofa stirring the air with his snores, and both Matilda and Darren are out back sipping tea and enjoying a game of Scrabble.

Everything came out in the following two months. The elderly man with terminal cancer, who was in such terrible pain that evening at the singing, had been pressing his button and dispensing nothing more than water, not the morphine he'd so desperately needed. Dr. Kwan had forgotten to take the old bottle of prescription pills from Mitzi's room, which was a huge mistake since Darren had discovered the empty capsules. Kwan had also paid Chester to follow me to Maple Gap and leave the note in my bag.

The powder I'd gathered from the handles of the treadmill turned out to be digoxin as Sue Mie had suspected. That, along with the colored sugar pills and empty capsules I'd gleaned from the bathroom in the back hall, served to pull the rope tighter around the necks of Dr. Kwan and Otis Payne. Confronted with the evidence, they finally confessed to stealing narcotics and other drugs to sell for profit.

The reason it had taken so long to find Otis when

the police arrived was because he'd been busy swapping T61 for another treadmill in storage. He'd asked Chester to make sure not to let anyone into that room, even offering him a bonus, though Chester said he had no idea about Polly's fall resulting from the poison on the handles.

And it was Otis who'd come into the bathroom that day Hardy and I hid in the shower. Seems he was trying to cover Dr. Kwan's slip in leaving Mitzi's old medication bottle with the empty capsules behind. Hardy and I congratulated Darren on noticing the bottles after the arrest of Dr. Kwan and Otis.

Louise Payne knew of their dealings and was blackmailing Otis to get a cut of the money. Otis dragged Hilda into the scheme with the promise of a cut of the money and asked her to mislabel some snacks dispensed to diabetics on the second floor. His thought had been to lay the blame of Polly's death on whatever CNA happened to be on the floor that evening handing out the snacks. He would report the mistake and say it caused Polly to get dizzy and fall, leading to a heart attack. Knowing she didn't have family to order an autopsy made him feel sure her history would help the police swallow that. Another juicy tidbit: Hilda was the one Otis was on the phone with the day Hardy and I were in the office with him and Sue Mie, not Louise.

Otis Payne did indeed let Polly into the gym that evening and directed her to the treadmill Dr. Kwan had already laced with digoxin, telling her to get started and promising Dr. Kwan would be in shortly for her evaluation. He knew all along the exercise and sweating would help the poison absorb through her skin that much faster. He'd waited just long enough in the room to know she was falling for the scheme. So the fall didn't kill her. Digoxin did. Just in case, Dr. Kwan had been prepared to finish her off with a syringe full of the stuff, and he'd waited in the back hallway to make good and sure she was dead.

Polly had stumbled on Dr. Kwan's narcotics-stealing scheme—neither Otis nor Dr. Kwan knew exactly how—but she tried to blackmail Dr. Kwan with what she knew. Getting closer to Otis was her way of making Kwan think she was going to tell unless he paid up. Of course, she didn't know Otis was in on the whole thing. Playing her games with Kwan only prompted the two villains to hatch their dastardly scheme to kill her.

Sue Mie was proud of her part in busting the scheme. She'd admitted to having a grudge against Otis for the "accident" that had befallen her uncle and having taken the job as CNA in hopes of finding proof that Otis Payne cut corners. Her frustration with Otis was also the reason she called the police after Polly's fall, to get back at him for her uncle's fall that, in her mind, was no accident. We keep in touch now, and I send her care packages for her two little boys.

Mitzi's poems had been scarily on target. I wondered just how much she truly had seen, and I figured Otis and Dr. Kwan probably didn't pay her much attention even if she had spied on them since they knew she wouldn't be a reliable witness.

Hardy and I found a new place for Matilda and Darren, who both wanted to move from Bridgeton

Towers. Can't say we blame them. Being that Momma and Darren have become such good friends, we made sure to find a place they both loved.

We're still not sure what will happen to Thomas since he admitted to pulling the emergency key. Hardy and I promised him we'd help him out if we could. Gertrude will no doubt prove a character witness for him, should the need arise.

As for me, the results are in. Test results, that is. Seems I've got me a good case of diabetes. It almost killed me to hear those words. The doctor reassured me I could control it without insulin for now, but I needed to think about changing my diet. Hardy chuckled at that one, until I banged him on his leg with my purse. But the sparkle was still in his eyes. When I let loose that a diet for me meant none of his favorites anymore, he sure lost the sass. I dragged him along to some support group meetings where we learned all kinds of useful information.

Still, the diabetes couldn't have happened at a worse time, what with Hardy and me in the process of buying Your Goose Is Cooked, the restaurant we've been talking about for the last few months. But we're looking forward to a new adventure as owners, and I'll stir up some healthy things, maybe even a salad or two. Who knows? Interpreted, Doc's diet change means losing weight, so I have great motivation to cook up some new healthy treats.

Lela is working at the boutique in Maple Gap, taking good care of Sara in her off hours. Sara's growing weaker daily. I can't bear to watch this baby slipping away. Her momma and I are in constant touch, and I'm praying mighty hard that the Good Lord will bundle her up close to Him. I've never had to face losing a child and can't imagine even touching the sharpness of that pain, but I do what I can to help others in small ways.

Hardy and I are going to slip away to visit little Arianna in the next couple of months before we open the restaurant, since we know managing that place will be full-time until we can get someone dependable to be cook and manager in our absence. Oh, and there're those new grandbabies coming soon.

S. Dionne Moore writes the LaTisha Barnhart Mystery series; LaTisha is the creator. Together they inspire one another to greatness, both in faith and fiction. S. Dionne can still do an entire week of laundry in a day. . .aren't you impressed? Besides writing, she is also a choir director, homeschooler, and the sole organizer of organization. Born and raised in Northern Virginia, she is a city girl with a small-town heart transplant who no longer has to take antirejection drugs! You can read more about her at her Web site, www.sdionnemoore.com.

You may correspond with this author by writing:
S. Dionne Moore
Author Relations
PO Box 721
Uhrichsville, OH 44683